LOVE BEYOND WANTING

BOOK 10 OF MORNA'S LEGACY SERIES

BETHANY CLAIRE

Editor: Dj Hendrickson
Cover Designed by Damonza

Available In eBook, Paperback, & Hardback

eBook ISBN: 978-1-947731-58-5
Paperback ISBN: 978-1-947731-59-2
Hardback ISBN: 978-1-947731-60-8

For Winston, Bash, Charlie, & Flag.

I couldn't ask for better writing companions.

A NOTE FROM THE AUTHOR

Dear Reader,

I am so pleased that you've picked up this copy of *Love Beyond Wanting*. I really enjoyed writing these characters. If you've been a fan of Morna's Legacy Series novels for a while and have read all the way through *Love Beyond Words*, feel free to skip the rest of this note and jump into reading this story. If you're new to Morna's world, however, I strongly suggest that you backtrack a bit before you dive in.

We've entered a new chapter in my Morna's stories, and with *Love Beyond Words* as the starting point, have begun a new story arc that will carry us through this novel and several subsequent novels. These books, which chronicle the legend of The Isle of Eight Lairds and the strong-willed women that Morna pulls together to defeat the evil that lives there, are more interconnected than any of my previous books. While the love stories themselves are standalones, the over-arching legend overlaps and weaves in and out of each story. For the most pleasurable reading experience, you should read *Love Beyond Words* before beginning this novel.

And for the complete picture, start at the beginning with *Love Beyond Time* and read every book in the series straight through. I know that most of my readers would say that this is by far the most enjoyable way to go about the series. You can find a complete reading order list on my website.

Okay, I think that's it. However you choose to read my novels, it is my sincerest hope that you love them.

Best wishes and happy reading,

Bethany

PROLOGUE

*M*any Years Before The Start of Our Story
The Isle of Whispers, Scotland

Machara couldn't be trusted. She was the worst sort of fae, but what else did Athdara have to lose? With her son as he was now, he had no life at all. With the body of an old man and the mind of a child, the boy would wither and die long before she would, and whatever time her son had left would be lived in misery. He couldn't speak, could barely feed himself, and rather than be rocked to sleep as a child his age should be, Willy was forced to cry himself to sleep, for he was too large to be held in her arms.

He was just a wee tot when she lost him, barely teetering about and just learning his first words. She'd known the moment he was gone who'd taken him. A week earlier, the baker's son had been lured into the world invisible to mortal eyes by a faerie. While Athdara had warned her young niece—begged her—to keep her son away from the spot where the first lad had

1

disappeared, the girl's curiosity was too strong. Just like the boy before, she was lured into the land of the fae with Athdara's wee son in tow.

The children were only gone a fortnight before the Isle's well-meaning laird struck a devil's bargain with the faerie Machara. But as faeries always do, she found a way to twist her word. Return the children she did, but not as they were before. Their bodies had aged decades in a matter of days, but their minds remained those of children.

"I know ye hate me."

Athdara reared back and spit on the ground near the faerie's feet. "Hate is too kind a word for what I feel for ye, Machara. My son was an innocent. He wasna old enough to be fooled by yer charms. What happened to him was no fault of his own. Ye might as well have killed him. He'd be better off dead."

The faerie's expression didn't change. Athdara knew Machara was incapable of feeling remorse. She knew that for Machara to offer her a bargain, there had to be something in it for her, as well. In order to get what she so desperately wanted, Athdara would have to outwit someone far older and more powerful than she.

"Aye, I know. 'Tis why I've offered ye this and ye alone. I must hide my son from his father, and he canna live amongst the fae. My own father would kill the boy if I brought him into our realm."

The child was no more than four—a wisp of a boy with curly honey-colored hair and shimmering green eyes that showed his half-fae blood more than any of his other features. He looked frightened standing next to his mother, shaking in the cold. Athdara watched as the boy reached for his mother's hand, only to be swatted away by Machara's spindly fingers. The boy's eyes began to fill with tears, and Athdara's heart squeezed.

"Why canna the boy see Nicol? Nicol wouldna harm him."

A lump rose in Athdara's throat as Machara laughed. Her cackle dripped with poison.

"Do ye think I care for the welfare of this child? I wanted a half-fae child so I could use him when it suited me later in life. These children have abilities that others will never know. I may need him if my father's curse comes true. If I gave him to Nicol, the child would grow up poisoned against me, and that willna do for my purposes."

Athdara wanted nothing more than to reach for the young boy and gather him up in her arms. Machara was a fool. The boy was old enough to remember all of this. She could see the child's heart breaking right in front of her. It would take no prompting for the young boy to grow up hating his mother. Machara had already done all the work necessary to plant that seed of hate in his heart.

"And what of yer other children?"

"I returned to Nicol's bed for the pleasure of it, not because I wanted more of his children. Those wretched beings willna be long for this world."

Athdara had to swallow the vomit that threatened to spill from her at Machara's confession. "Doona harm them, Machara. Give them to me, just as ye are doing with this boy, and I will care for them as well."

Machara's brow lifted. "I will use each of my children for a purpose that suits me. Brachan must live. The others must die. If ye speak of them again, I will take my bargain to someone else. 'Tis time for ye to decide, Athdara. Do ye accept my offer or not?"

Carefully, and with a heavy heart, Athdara prepared her words. It was clear to her that she couldn't save Machara's other children. If the faerie wished them dead, she was powerless against the evil fae's will, but perhaps she could spare one of them, and in the process, regain her son.

"If ye will see my Willy returned perfect and whole and to the same age he truly should be now, with no memory of what happened to him, and if ye promise me that ye will never interfere in my life again or look for me or any of my kin or offspring, and ye willna interfere in how I choose to raise yer child, then aye. I shall take the boy in as my own, and I shall leave this isle with him."

Machara smiled and Athdara sent up a silent prayer that she'd left no room for Machara to trick her.

"Then we've reached an agreement."

Before Athdara could move, Machara reached for Willy's wrinkled and twisted hand. As she gripped him, his appearance changed before Athdara's eyes. As her young son returned to the bonny toddler he'd once been, she collapsed on the ground, pulled him into her arms, and wept.

As she held her son, Machara shoved Brachan toward her, and Athdara gathered him in her embrace, as well.

"Leave here now, Machara. Yer need of me is done."

Machara nodded, but didn't leave. "Aye, 'tis. I shall call for my son when 'tis time—when he is grown, not before, as per our bargain."

"How will ye call for him?"

"He will know. There will be an awakening within him that he willna be able to deny. When this happens, ye must tell him who he is and to whom he belongs and return him to me once more. If ye doona do so, I will kill yer son."

Shivering, Athdara gripped each child's hand and rose from the ground. "And what makes ye think that I willna poison Brachan toward ye like ye say Nicol would've? Ye've already sworn that ye willna interfere with how I raise the lad."

Machara laughed, but Athdara could see the faerie's fatal flaw.

"Ye are not his blood. Yer words will have no pull on him. As he grows, he will see ye as little more than the woman who saw him fed and clothed. His loyalty will lie with those whose blood runs through his veins."

Athdara waited until Machara was gone, but once the faerie was out of sight, she laughed. How little Machara knew of humans and love. Blood means little. Family comes from the heart. And this boy—this half-fae rarity—would grow up to be kind and good and brave—nothing like Machara.

He would be her son, and she would love him completely.

CHAPTER 1

*B*oston, Massachusetts—*Present Day*

*M*y alarm didn't wake me—I'd turned that off hours ago after realizing with delight that the one and only good thing about Laurel being in Scotland was that she wasn't around to bully me into going to therapy. After this many months, I figured it was acceptable to skip one time. In my mind, it was the biggest waste of an hour each week anyway. But rather than enjoy a lazy morning in bed with my cat, my phone dinged at seven-thirty a.m. on the dot with a text message from my rehabilitation therapist, Sue.

> *Laurel called before she left for Scotland. I know she's not there to get you up and around. If Dr. Ackard doesn't call me at 10:00 to tell me you were at your session, I'll not be at ours at 11:30. See you in a few hours! :-)*

Groaning, I stretched and reached down to pat Mr. Crinkles, my solid black, one-eyed, relentlessly ornery cat who lay curled up on the far corner of my bed. He began to purr.

Ever since the fire that took my right arm and my cat's left eye, Laurel and Sue had embodied the very definition of "tough-love." Even immediately following the accident, when I was still in unbearable pain and wading through tremendous grief over losing my arm, Laurel wouldn't do a thing for me. She wanted me to do everything on my own. Even when I threw self-pity-fueled temper tantrums—which happened more often in those first few months than I cared to admit—she never caved.

Sue was no different in my sessions with her. She pushed me to my breaking point every week. As a result, each week I grew stronger. I owed both of them so much, but that didn't mean I wasn't still incredibly pissed to get her unwelcome text message at—what was for me—the ass-crack of dawn.

It was the one part of her work with me that drove me mad. Sue was the best rehabilitation therapist in Boston, but she would only accept clients who agreed to see a counselor each and every week while under her care. In theory, I understood her reasoning. Most of her clients were recovering from terrible accidents or illnesses and were learning to work with the body they now had. Of course there were psychological issues that needed to be worked through after such a tragedy.

But what Sue didn't seem to understand or believe, no matter how many times I tried to tell her, was that I had already worked through all of my feelings about the accident. It had happened. It was awful. It was time for me to move the hell on.

"Knock knock." In her signature style that wasn't really knocking, my mother *knocked* on the door by saying the words out loud while she pushed the door open without permission. "I brought coffee."

I smiled and scooted myself up in the bed. Despite my insistence that I didn't need her help, Mom had flown up to Boston from her home in Florida the day after Laurel left for Scotland. She'd been showering me with attention, and I'd be a liar if I said I wasn't milking it just a little bit. So many of the things Laurel would never do for me, Mom would, and since it delighted her so much to feel like she was helping me, I allowed it. Or at least, that's the excuse I made for myself when I started to feel guilty for letting her do things that I was entirely capable of doing on my own.

"How did you know I was up?"

"I didn't. If you weren't, I was going to wake you. While you were showering yesterday morning, Dr. Ackard's office called to confirm your appointment this morning. I told them you would be there."

Silently, I took the cup of coffee as I watched Mr. Crinkles lean into my mom and begin to purr. He was such a ham.

"What if I wasn't going to be there?"

Her scrunched brows made her look as if she didn't understand the question. "Of course you're going to be there. Sue won't see you otherwise, and you can't afford to miss one of your sessions with her."

"Sure I can. All we're working on now is strength and range of motion in my shoulder. I can work on those things from home."

Mom continued as if she couldn't hear me speaking. "I made eggs Benedict again—your favorite."

She'd made it every morning since arriving. While it was indeed my favorite meal, I didn't have the heart to tell her I'd tired of it days ago.

"Thank you. You really don't have to cook for me every morning. Sometimes, a bowl of cereal would be just fine."

She smiled and waved a dismissive hand as she stood and turned toward the door.

"It's no trouble. I enjoy doing it."

She paused as she reached the door and looked down at the mess of open books I had spread out over my desk. "What's all this?"

I couldn't possibly tell her all that I was researching, all that Laurel was up to, or the fact that my sister was most likely chilling in the seventeenth century. "It's nothing. Just doing some research. Trying to brainstorm ideas for Laurel's next book."

She twisted her head to the side and looked at me skeptically. "Laurel's next book?"

I nodded and she shook her head as she exhaled sadly. "You shouldn't miss your counseling sessions, Kate. Not even once. Why don't you hop in the shower? We can eat before you leave for your appointment."

She left without another word, leaving me confused and wondering why my explanation of the books spread out on my desk had caused her to tell me I shouldn't miss counseling.

At least now I had something to talk about in today's session.

"*W*hat do you think your mother meant by that statement, Kate?"

I sighed and leaned back rather dramatically in my chair. "Please don't do that. Don't say the most therapy-sounding thing you could possibly say when I really do want your opinion. If I knew what she meant by it, I wouldn't have spent all morning wondering what she meant by it."

She pinched her lips together as if contemplating whether or not to tell me what she was really thinking. "Why didn't you simply ask her what she meant by it?"

"I suppose I knew that if I did, she would give me some sort of non-answer and it would aggravate me and then we'd get into an argument."

"Or maybe you were worried that she would tell you exactly what she meant by it and that would aggravate you even more?"

"See?" I pointed at her. "That's why I don't like therapists. You clearly believe you know what she meant by it, but you won't tell me. You'd rather torture me by trying to make me figure it out on my own."

Dr. Ackard looked as if it was taking every muscle in her face to suppress an eye roll at my dramatics. "I am not trying to torture you, Kate. I just don't want to answer the question because I don't know your mother. I don't know what she meant by the statement. You do know her."

"Okay, fine." I paused as I tried to think of another way to approach this with her. "You also believe that I shouldn't skip therapy every week. So, why don't you tell me why you believe that? Why do I need to be here so badly? I don't feel like I'm in a bad place anymore. I feel pretty stable and sound of mind."

She shifted in her seat but kept her expression calm and collected. "First of all, of course you are stable and sound of mind. Most people who seek counseling are and it's offensive for you to suggest otherwise. *Everyone* needs help working through things in their life now and again."

I smiled, feeling vindicated. "That's my point though. I feel as if I've worked through this difficult thing. I feel as if I'm past it."

Dr. Ackard shrugged and crossed her arms. "Perhaps you are. I really wouldn't know."

"What does that mean? I'm in here with you every week. You should know better than anyone."

She gave me one curt nod and lifted a hand in concession. "You're right. I should, but I really know nothing about you, Kate. I know a whole lot about your sister's dating life and your efforts to see her set up via a whole host of online dating sites and disasters. I know a lot about your mother. I know that you loved your job before the fire, but I have no idea how you feel about it now. And now, I know a lot about your sister's trip to Scotland and your desire to research her location, that I don't quite understand, but I know nothing about you."

I didn't understand her. Despite my weekly reluctance to attend my counseling sessions with her, I spoke to her the whole hour each and every time. I'd talked about all sorts of things over the weeks and months with her.

"But all of those things are about me."

"No, Kate. They're about the people close to you. You never talk about yourself. And whenever I ask you about anything related directly to you, you get squirmy."

My clothes felt suddenly too tight as my defensiveness grew.

"I do not."

"How was your last date with Dillon? What do you think of his suggestion that you move out of Kate's apartment and in with him?"

Dillon had nothing to do with this. I glanced at the clock.

"I think I've already gone over my hour."

"My next appointment cancelled. It's fine if we go over."

I stood and moved toward the door. "I have to get to Sue's. It takes a while from here. See you next week, Dr. Ackard."

She called after me as I reached the door. "Kate."

I paused with my hand on the handle.

"Surely you can see that you've just proven my point. I'm

here for you as long as you need me, but you're never going to make any progress until you are willing to stop distracting yourself with anything and everything outside of yourself. First, it was getting Dillon set up in his dental practice, then it was Laurel's dating life, now it's Laurel's trip to Scotland. Someday you're going to have to deal with you."

I left without a word. Sue wouldn't have to push me at all today. I was too frustrated and fired up. I had more than enough energy to do whatever she asked me to.

CHAPTER 2

The Scottish Mainland—1651

"What do ye imagine they're up to?" Harry chuckled before continuing, "I know what I'd do if I had the castle to myself with a lass as bonny as Laurel as my only company. I wouldna leave my bedchamber. Not until the lot of ye returned and forced me out of it."

Three days on the mainland and there was still no sign of Calder. Maddock knew Harry only spoke in such a way to distract himself from all that was on his mind—no one worried over Calder's departure more than Harry.

"If Raudrich heard ye speak of Laurel like that, he'd bloody yer nose."

Nicol, their Master and the castle's resident nocturne, snorted quietly but, as usual, said nothing.

Harry's face flushed red as he sheepishly looked downward to apologize. "Ach, ye know I meant no disrespect to the lass."

"Aye, I know, and I know what I'd be doing, as well, but Raudrich is daft. I willna be surprised if we return home to see that they are no closer to one another in body or mind. He still hasna told Laurel that he loves her when 'tis plain to everyone that he does."

Harry looked over at him with surprise. "Raudrich may know how he feels but 'tis no surprise that he's not told her yet. They hardly know one another. The lass hasna been at the castle all that long."

Maddock shook his head in dismissal. Laurel was an easy lass to love. He suspected that every man in the castle, save Calder, was halfway in love with her, but none of them held her heart as Raudrich did.

"Do ye think time matters with a lass like that? For so long, the lot of us have been isolated from the world outside of our castle. If given the chance to give my love to another as bonny as Laurel, I'd not hesitate a moment."

They rode in silence for a moment with Nicol trailing a short distance behind them. Eventually, Harry spoke again.

"Would ye really, Maddock? Even with our destinies already fated? Would ye start a family there at the castle, knowing that ye may never truly leave the Isle? Would ye do so with Machara there?"

"Machara willna be there forever. With time, we will defeat her. She will die, and someday, we will all be free."

Maddock had no real reason to believe as he did, but it was a belief he never questioned. If he did, he knew his hope would crumble like wet parchment, and he had too many people to protect to allow that to happen.

Harry let out a grumble and shook his head. "I wish I believed as ye do, Maddock. 'Twould be a nice dream to allow myself now and again." His friend paused, then sheepishly continued, "But mayhap dreams do come true. One has for Raudrich in Laurel. The lass couldna suit him anymore perfectly."

Maddock agreed, but God how he envied him. "Aye. I doona envy Raudrich her. Laurel is a friend, and we couldna ever be more, but I do envy him the bond he's found with her. Mayhap we should ask Laurel if she's any sisters or friends she could invite to the Isle."

He laughed at the thought. How different things would be for all of them if more women suddenly entered their life.

"Aye, I doona know of friends, but she does have a sister."

"What?" Maddock couldn't believe that he didn't know that. Raudrich was the only person at the castle who'd spent more time with Laurel than he. The two of them had formed a fast friendship, though clearly, they'd not yet gotten to know one another as well as he believed they had.

"Does she really? Did she tell ye that?"

"No, she dinna. Marcus mentioned her. He said that he and Laurel were forced to end their last trip to Scotland early after Laurel's sister was caught in a fire."

"Was she..." Maddock hesitated. "Did the lass live?"

"Aye, though she was gravely injured. I believe he mentioned something about the lass losing her arm."

Maddock shuddered as old, dreaded memories flashed through his mind. "When I was five, I saw a man burned alive. The sight of him, the sound of his screams, and that god-awful smell..." He shuddered. "I wouldna wish such a fate on anyone."

"Not even Machara?"

Even the evil fae that kept them all bound to the Isle didn't deserve such a fate.

"Not even Machara. Where is her sister now?"

Harry shrugged and nudged his horse to move more quickly.

"I doona know, but I expect 'twillna be long before we see her. I doona believe Laurel and Marcus are going anywhere, and Laurel doesna seem like the sort of lass who would be content to be separated from her family."

The idea of meeting Laurel's sister excited Maddock more than he was willing to admit—especially right now with Calder still missing and Machara's threat looming larger than ever before.

"Aye, and if she's half as bonny as Laurel..." he trailed off as Harry laughed and spoke just a short distance ahead of him.

"Aye, I believe she is. Marcus said she's verra striking."

"O'course, she is."

He'd not yet met her and he could already sense he was in trouble.

CHAPTER 3

*P*resent Day

*I*t was exactly five-thirty in the morning when I finally cast aside any remaining doubt that all of this was real. After stewing over my therapist's parting words for the better part of the day, I returned to Laurel's apartment more ready than ever to dive back into the research I'd been obsessed over since the moment Laurel left for Scotland. Mr. Crinkles lay curled up on the far corner of my bed, surrounded by the empty wrappers of one-ounce pieces of chocolate that I'd recklessly strewn over the top of my mattress. Over the six-plus-hour study session, I'd nearly eaten my weight in chocolate. The candy, combined with the extra-large thermos of coffee I'd guzzled, had me near caffeine overdose. My feet seemed to bounce on their own as I reviewed my sources one more time. The book on The Isle of Eight Lairds, which had mysteriously appeared in my sister's path, was now excessively highlighted and worn from use.

The four credible websites I'd found on the subject were all open on different tabs of my web browser for easy reference, and the recorded documentary was paused on its most fascinating part on my bedroom television.

The movement of my feet shook the bed. Mr. Crinkles stirred, opened his one green eye, and glared at me as if to say, *Stop it, human, or I will cut you.* He would, too. He could leap faster than I could move out of the way, and his claws were like little razor blades. The moment I stopped fidgeting, he closed his eye and went back to sleep. Careful not to disturb him again, I pushed myself slowly off the bed so I could burn off the excess caffeine by pacing the room.

I'd combed through every page of the book three times, watched the documentary on the subject twice, and knew every word on each of these web pages by heart. Each and every source held some piece of information that made it impossible to deny what my heart already knew. My sister and her best friend, Marcus, truly were in the past. They were both meant to be there. And—if the book's footnote about a marred woman, along with one very quick mention of a one-eyed black cat in the documentary was to be believed—so were Mr. Crinkles and I.

Every bit of it was absurd, but I knew in my bones it was true.

I paced back and forth for the better part of an hour, until I heard the quiet movements of my mother in the kitchen. Knowing that I couldn't take another day of eggs Benedict, I took a quick glance in the mirror and rumpled up the sleeves of my pajamas so it would look like I'd just rolled out of bed before I went to the kitchen to stop her. She couldn't have looked more surprised to see me up and about.

"Kate. Did I wake you? I thought I might run over to the

gym down the street and get a short workout in, but if you're up, I can go ahead and make you breakfast first."

I walked past her to the cabinet and reached inside to grab a box of cereal.

"No need. Honestly, just something simple will be perfect this morning. Enjoy your workout."

There was something resembling guilt in her expression as she left, and I quickly took on the feeling myself.

Everything that I'd learned overnight affected her, as well, and I'd done a remarkable job keeping it from her. If Laurel and I were destined to live in the past, surely she was, too. We were her world. She couldn't bear being away from us forever. And if my mother would have to come with me, then surely David would have to, as well. Marcus' dad was as attached to his son as our mother was to us.

Overwhelmed and slightly dizzy from all the caffeine and sugar, I set the box of cereal down on the counter and went to the bathroom and turned on the shower. There was so much I needed to do, and I didn't have a clue where to start. A nice, long, hot shower was in order to get me prepped and ready for the very busy day ahead.

I needed to take care of everything as quickly as possible.

Otherwise, I knew I'd talk myself out of it.

The shower was a disaster. The hot water helped clear my head, but doing so only made room for all of the doubts and questions my research had unearthed to come rushing to the forefront of my mind. None of it made sense. Even if somehow it was all possibly true, what was I supposed to do about it? By the time I got out of the shower and wrapped a towel around my body, I was shaking with anxiety. The moment I stepped back into my bedroom, there was a knock at the door.

Looking through the peephole I saw an elderly woman smiling up at the door.

"Umm...hold on just a moment, ma'am. Let me put on some clothes."

Her gaze flickered to the peephole. I swear she could actually see me.

"Ach, no need, lass. I know what a naked woman looks like. I've the same bits myself. Though nowadays, they're a little softer and droopier than yers are, I reckon. Open the door. I need to speak with ye this instant, before yer mother returns."

Suspicion washed through me, and I found myself hoping that she was who I so desperately needed her to be.

"Who...who are you?"

"Lass, ye know who I am. 'Tis Morna. Open the door, please."

Pinching the towel closed with what was left of my right arm, I glanced down to make sure I was covered and opened the door. She stepped inside without hesitation and had no qualms about making herself at home.

"'Tis a lovely apartment. Ye decorated it, aye? Ye have wonderful taste."

"Yes, I did." I stared after her with a sense of astonishment. I'd spent days trying to piece things together. I couldn't believe she was here.

"I'm sure ye are wondering why I'm here."

I laughed uncomfortably as I wondered if she'd read my thoughts. "Yes, though I really am pleased to see you. I have a lot of questions for you."

She nodded and moved to sit down on the couch. "Aye, and I'll answer what I can. First though, do ye have any tea?"

Nodding, I went to turn on the kettle of water and get us a couple of cups. By the time I returned to the living room, Mr. Crinkles was curled up in Morna's lap, purring like crazy.

"Kate, who is this handsome young man in the photo with ye and Laurel?"

Mr. Crinkles watched me with his one green eye as I moved to sit across from Morna.

"That would be my boyfriend, Dillon."

She narrowed her eyes suspiciously at me and said nothing for a long moment. When she did speak, her tone was admonishing. "I dinna see him while watching ye. Not at all."

"You've been watching me?"

"Aye."

"Well, I haven't seen him in a few days. We're supposed to go out tonight."

"I doona mean visibly, lass. I mean in yer heart and mind. Ye doona think of him unless someone else brings him up. There are only two reasons a woman distracts herself from thinking of her man—either she loves him too little, or too much, and she doesna wish to experience how either of those realities make her feel. Which is it?"

As much as I didn't want to admit it, I knew it was this sort of thing my therapist had been talking about. Thinking about Dillon made me uncomfortable. So, most of the time, I didn't think about him. I enjoyed my time with him when we were together, but I never felt as if my life was missing anything when he wasn't around. If Morna was right, and there were only two reasons that I would distract myself in such a way, I knew it wasn't from loving him too much.

It must've taken me too long to answer. For after a brief moment, Morna gently leaned forward and placed a hand on my knee.

"Ye should let him go, lass. Yer life is about to get much more complicated. If ye doona love him, there is no room for him along this new path."

For the first time in months, I felt tears threaten to build up in my eyes. I quickly shook my head to push them away.

"How is Laurel? Is she really in the past?"

Morna righted herself as she nodded and gently began stroking Mr. Crinkles' back. I couldn't believe he was sitting there so contentedly.

"Aye. She'll be calling ye tonight. 'Tis why I needed to speak with ye this morning."

"Calling me? From the seventeenth century?"

"Aye. I sent her a way to speak with ye, for I canna speak with her myself."

"Why?"

"Because she would ask for my help, and I would be too tempted to give it, which I canna do. 'Twould doom not only her but every man that lives in the castle with her."

I repeated the same question. "Why is that?"

Morna sighed, and I could sense that whatever she was about to tell me had been weighing on her for some time. "Ye've done a fine job of piecing things together, but there is one piece yer information got wrong."

"Just one piece? If that's all, then I'm pleasantly surprised. Which part was wrong?"

"The prophecy given to Machara by her father was no prophecy. It was a curse. He dinna tell her what *was* to be, only what *could* be. He cast into existence a way for her to be defeated —a way to end her immortality."

I thought back on all I'd read about faeries over the past days, and Morna's revelation made sense. Faeries didn't die easily, if ever, and all that I'd read indicated that, at some point,

Machara would—or perhaps the right word was *could*—be defeated.

"Why would her own father create a way for her to die?"

"I canna tell ye that, lass. All that I know, I learned from a friend long ago. He is no longer around to give us any more answers than we already have."

Something sad flashed in Morna's eyes at the mention of her friend, but she quickly masked it with a smile when she noticed my stare.

"This friend...is he the reason you're involved with this at all?"

"Aye. I often meddle in the lives of my kinsmen, but not verra often do I meddle in the lives of strangers. I share no blood with any on The Isle of Eight Lairds, but I made a promise to one who does that I would help in the only way Machara's father's curse would allow."

She paused and I allowed the silence to linger between us. I sensed she was readying herself for a longer story.

"Raudrich—yer sister's beau—is the grandson of a man who once loved me verra much. Long after I'd left the time I was born in, I sensed Hamish calling to me in my sleep. He was near death and needed to see me one last time, so I went to him. On his deathbed, I learned of Machara and the havoc she'd wreaked on The Isle of Whispers.

"Hamish was devastated that his young grandson had been called to a life of such restriction. Raudrich's powers made it necessary that he become one of The Eight, but Hamish dinna want the boy to be trapped in a life without choice. He couldna leave the curse to chance, so he asked me to use my skill to gather a group of women strong enough to defeat her."

The details of the curse ran through my mind. Suddenly, I understood.

"But you can't tell us how, can you? Because you're not entirely mortal, and Machara can only be defeated by mortal women."

Morna's whole posture relaxed as she leaned back into the chair and let out a big sigh.

"Precisely, lass. 'Tis not that I doona wish to help Laurel, 'tis only that if there is to be hope for any of ye, I canna do so."

"All you can do is get us each back there and leave the rest to history."

Morna's eyebrows scrunched together in what I could only describe as a look of concern.

"Aye, and no, lass. Aye, all I can do is get ye back there, but suggesting that any of us 'leave the rest to history' makes it seem as if the end result is predestined. That insinuates that ye have nothing to worry about."

That was honestly my understanding of the situation. The stories about the Isle were already legendary—history already knew how this would turn out.

"Isn't it? If not, how can you explain the books and the documentary?"

Morna laughed and shook her head, which immediately worried me. "That would be nice, aye? But alas, time is much more fluid than ye are capable of understanding. 'Tis verra possible, in truth 'tis verra likely, that Machara will best one or many of ye. If she does, if ye doona defeat her, then the stories and documentaries ye've seen in yer time will simply change to match what happens then. Nothing is set, Kate. How this turns out is up to each of ye lassies who will face her. All I can do is choose worthy opponents for her and keep my fingers crossed that each of ye are as brave and wise as ye seem to be."

"I'm beginning to think I would've preferred not knowing all of this before I went back."

She stood and began to walk toward the door.

"Ye needed to know. Yer faith in how ye believed things would turn out would've made ye reckless. Fear, in this case, is good. But doona ever doubt yer bravery, Kate. Ye have that in spades. Now, I must be on my way, but I need to tell ye a few last things. First, I know that yer mother and David must come, and I believe that is fine, though 'tis up to ye how ye plan on getting them there. Second, I would welcome ye at my inn and would be happy to send ye back via my spell, but when yer sister calls ye tonight, she shall offer ye a better way. Such a journey willna only be easier, but 'twill allow ye to be surrounded by people who can help yer mother and David adjust to the shock of what they will learn when they get there. Either way, I've no doubt that we will see each other again."

She leaned in to kiss my cheek in farewell, and then paused as she started to pull away.

"One last thing, doona tell Laurel I was here. Feign ignorance to anything she tells ye that coincides with what we have discussed. She still has her battle to fight. It willna do for her to know I was here."

I agreed and watched her until she was safely outside my building.

It seemed a very long way to travel for a conversation that could easily have been had on the phone, but then again, for a time-traveling witch, I supposed the journey from Scotland to Boston was no trouble at all.

CHAPTER 4

om didn't return home from the gym until nearly eleven, which while surprising, actually worked out for the best. It allowed me to form a plan and actually slip away for a bit myself to take care of a few of the many loose ends that would have to be tied up within the next few weeks.

After Morna left and I finished getting ready for the day, I decided to take care of the most obvious piece of business first. I went to my downtown office for the first time since the fire and began to disassemble the pieces of my life in Boston as quickly as I could. Otherwise, I knew I would collapse in a giant puddle of tears.

While many of my clients had moved on to other interior designers after my accident, there were a handful of gracious souls who'd insisted that I hold on to their deposits, take all the time I needed to heal, and then resume work on their projects when I was ready. The first thing I did upon walking into my office was call them, back out of the jobs, and place all of their deposits back in the mail to them.

Once that was done, I moved through the rest of my list as quickly as possible:

1. Cancel the lease on my office and see if I could get my deposit back. (Since I was pulling out four months early, they said no to the deposit.)

2. Research the cost of flights to Edinburgh and figure out a way to come up with the money. (Holy-freaking-crap! Flights are expensive. Maxed out credit cards would be my only option.)

3. Call Sue and tell her to cancel the order for the prosthetic. (She was immensely disappointed. She'd spent the last six weeks convincing me to begin working with one, but when I explained to her that it was because I was going to Scotland to visit Laurel, she seemed to perk up. While it was regrettable that she was under the impression that I'd be returning to Boston in a few weeks, I could see no other alternative than to mislead her.)

4. Figure out a story that would get both Mom and David to agree to a trip to Scotland. (This one took me much longer to figure out, and I wouldn't know until later that evening if my story was believable or not.)

5. Pack up my office and hire a couple of movers to help me move out. (I would have to call movers to help me pack boxes, as well. I spent the better part of two hours and ended up crying in frustration. There were many things—such as putting together boxes with only one arm—that I'd yet to master.)

After knocking off most of my list in just a few hours, I made it back to Laurel's apartment a half hour before Mom did. By the time she did arrive, I was slightly concerned.

"Did you just get back from the gym?"

She paused in the doorway and hesitated a little too long. "Uh, yes. I was just enjoying myself so much that I guess I lost track of time."

I stared at her as she turned her back to me to lock the door.

There were no females in our family that enjoyed exercise enough to get "carried away" with it. There was no way in hell she'd been at the gym this whole time, but I saw no reason to pry. She was grown, and so was I. We could both have our secrets.

"Hm. Okay, hey, I have something I wanted to ask you. Do you have plans tonight?"

She took a moment to hang her keys on one of the hooks by the front door then walked over to the couch and sat down next to me.

"Not at all. Are you wanting to get out of the house?"

I knew the question was really more of a suggestion. She and Laurel both believed that since the fire I'd isolated myself way too much, which was ridiculous coming from either one of them. They were world-class hermits.

"I was wondering if you could meet me for dinner at that really great Italian place close to my office? I'm going to ask David to come, too. I need to speak with both of you."

She made a startled, jerky motion with her head as if something I'd said frightened her. "David, as in Marcus' dad? Why does he need to come? Is everything okay? Are Laurel and Marcus in trouble?"

I should've known that her mind would immediately jump to some sort of tragedy.

"No, no, don't worry. Everything is totally fine. Laurel called while you were out. She wants me to surprise the two of you with something."

She still looked skeptical. "And this is a good something?"

I nodded. "Yes. I think you will think this is a very good something."

"Okay, then." She smiled, and I found that I was able to relax just a little bit although getting her to go and eat wasn't even close to being the most difficult part. If she was skeptical about me wanting to eat with her, she would be an impossibly hard sell on the concept of time travel.

I took a breath as I reminded myself that I just needed to take everything one step at a time.

"Perfect."

My phone buzzed on the coffee table, and I glanced down to see Dillon's name and photo pop up on the screen.

"Damnit." I cursed under my breath as I picked up the phone. I'd forgotten all about our date for tonight.

Mom stood, sensing that I needed privacy, and began to move away from the couch.

"You go ahead and answer that. I'll go in Laurel's room and call David to see if he can meet us tonight."

I'd almost answered until I heard what Mom meant to do.

"You'll call David? Do you even know David?"

She cocked her head to the side and crossed her arms in annoyance. "Of course I know David. It's no trouble for me to call him."

"Okay, well, thanks then."

I waited until she was inside Laurel's room before answering the phone. Dillon sounded so excited, and it made me feel wretched all over.

"Hey, babe. Just checking in to make sure everything is still set for tonight. I can't wait to see you. I have one tooth extraction and three fillings before I get to go home for the weekend. Is seven good for a pick-up time?"

I took a deep breath and tried to muster up some phlegm at the back of my throat. "Oh, Dillon," I coughed for effect. "I should've called you this morning. I'm sick. Really sick." I paused for more coughing. "I have to cancel."

"That sucks, Kate. I'm sorry. I...I would offer to come over, but I can't really afford to get sick right now."

I frowned, surprised that his reaction upset me. I wasn't even really sick, but if I had been, I'd have wished for more sympathy.

"Oh, of course not. We can't have that. I'll call you tomorrow."

He sighed. "Okay, babe. Get some rest. I love you."

"I love you too." It wasn't a lie, but it wasn't enough either.

CHAPTER 5

*M*y nerves began to get the best of me as I sat in the restaurant and waited for my mother and David to arrive. I'd not been able to completely finish with my office that morning, so rather than the two of us ride to the restaurant together, I'd spent the rest of the day downtown with a couple of movers packing things up.

They were both fifteen minutes late. While I didn't know David all that well, Mom was never late for anything.

Just as I reached for my phone, they walked into the restaurant together.

Swallowing my panic, I smiled and stood to greet them.

Mom didn't bother hugging me—she was doing enough of that at home. Instead, she just gave me a quick smile and sat down while David wrapped me up in the biggest hug I'd had in ages. Just like his son, David gave remarkably warm and wonderful hugs.

"You look good, Kate. How are you feeling?"

"Better. Most days I feel very good. I often still feel like that right arm is hanging around, but I'm told that's fairly common."

He smiled as he released me. His gaze couldn't hide his pity, but it was something I'd grown accustomed to. Strangers were actually easier than people I'd known before. Those who knew me before the fire—their eyes screamed pity. It was part of the reason that moving to the past didn't seem so daunting to me. At least there, nobody would be able to say they knew who I was before. They would only know me as I am now.

We sat down at the table as the waiter came to take our drink orders.

"Did you guys get stuck in the same traffic jam? I can't believe you showed up at the exact same time."

"We…" Mom hesitated and cast a quick glance in David's direction. "We rode together. David picked me up."

"Oh. That's…" I was so shocked I didn't know what to say. "That's economical of you."

My mother's tone was defensive when she answered. "Laurel and Marcus have been friends for most of their lives, Kate. David and I have known each other a very long time."

Her reaction confused me, but the way David softly cleared his throat as if to calm her baffled me even more. I could feel her getting agitated, and that was the very last sort of mood she needed to be in. I would sit around and ponder what could be going on with her later. For now, I knew I needed to lighten the mood.

"Okay, it's no problem. I think it's very nice that he offered to pick you up." I smiled to ease some of the tension. "So, I'm sure you guys are wondering why I asked you both to come eat."

My mother sighed and straightened up in her chair as she ran a hand through her long, dark, curly hair.

She was nervous, and I couldn't for the life of me figure out why.

David leaned forward and smiled. "Actually, we have a pretty good idea."

My mind immediately began to flip through everything I'd done today. How could they possibly know? "You do? How?"

Something in my mother's worried gaze shifted, and before David could answer, she shot out her arm to squeeze my hand.

"We visited on the way over here. We have our suspicions. Why don't you tell us what it is? Then we will tell you if we were right."

I couldn't stay up all night again tonight. My sleep-deprived brain was making it difficult for me to understand anything she was saying.

"Okay..." I started slowly as I carefully made sure to say everything exactly according to plan. "Well, it's nothing for either of you to worry about. It's a good thing."

David smiled. "We know."

I could feel my face shift into an expression of utter confusion, but before I could ask anything, Mom jumped in.

"Ignore him, Kate. Go ahead with what you were saying."

I nodded and reached to grab my water glass, taking a quick sip before continuing. "Shortly after I got to my office this morning, I got a call from Laurel. They've decided to stay in Scotland for the rest of the summer."

"Oh?"

I expected my mother to be stressed by the news. I knew she would feel the need to stay in Boston until Laurel returned, and such an extended trip would undoubtedly disrupt her life in Florida greatly, but the way her voice lifted at the end of her question made her seem rather pleased at the revelation.

I stared at her until she noticed my expression. "Are you okay, Mom?"

She answered—in my opinion—a little too quickly. "Of course I'm okay. Why wouldn't I be okay?"

I shrugged. "I just...I didn't expect you to be so pleased with the news. You don't really seem like yourself this afternoon."

"Of course, I'm pleased. If Laurel and Marcus are planning to stay the summer, then it must mean that they're having an excellent time. That's all any mother wants for her children—for them to be happy."

I had the strongest urge to whisper under my breath, *Maybe some mothers,* but I refrained. I knew, of course, that Mom did want that for both of us. She was often just too intense for that to show through.

Instead, I smiled, waited for the waiter to take our meal orders, and then once he was gone, continued with the rest of my plan.

"Well, good. If that makes you happy, I'm certain this will, as well. Since Laurel and Marcus have decided to stay the summer, and Marcus' thirtieth birthday is as at the end of July, they've invited the three of us to visit them. Laurel's treat."

David's eyes grew wide as he dropped the breadstick he'd been about to stick in his mouth. "You don't mean she's agreed to pay for it?"

I nodded excitedly. "That's exactly what I mean. She was really insistent. She told me to visit with you guys and for us to pick a date that would work for all of us, as soon as possible."

Mom's eyes welled up with tears. "Let's go now. First thing tomorrow. I can pack tonight."

David laughed and reached out to gently squeeze Mom's shoulder. "I would love to leave tomorrow, too, Myla, but I'm in the middle of the first summer session. The earliest I could possibly leave is three weeks, and that's only if I can get another professor to take over my second session summer course."

I couldn't deny being a little disappointed. My eagerness to leave was nearly equal with Mom's, but three weeks seemed sound. There were still many things I would have to take care of.

"But you do think you can find someone to take over next session's course?"

"Kate, if you'll book the flight, and Laurel's paying for my ticket, then I'll go with you one way or another. If I'm unable to find someone to cover it, I'll quit."

I could say nothing to him, but if I was right about all of this, quitting, whether he realized it or not, was exactly what David would be doing.

A flash of familiar dark hair and broad shoulders in the doorway caught my eye, and every ounce of blood drained from my face as I watched Dillon walk into the restaurant. I was directly in his line of vision. There was no way he wouldn't see me.

I briefly contemplated diving beneath the table, but his head turned my way before I could make the move. His eyelids did this odd fluttery thing as if he was trying to process what he was seeing, but then his gaze changed to one of anger. I knew I had no option but to go to him and face this situation head on.

"Excuse me for a second. Dillon is here, and I need to speak with him."

"Dillon!" Mom nearly jumped out of her chair in excitement. She loved Dillon—probably more than I did. "Invite him over."

Shakily, I lay my napkin down on the table and stood.

"I don't think he's in the mood to talk, Mom. I told him I was sick. He didn't know we were going to be here."

She looked horrified.

"Why would you do that?"

"It doesn't matter. You two finish your meal. I'm going to take Dillon back to his apartment. See you in a bit."

Dillon's expression was unlike any I'd ever seen on him, but he kept himself collected in the restaurant as I approached him.

"You lied."

"I know. Why don't we walk back to your apartment? We need to talk."

CHAPTER 6

"*N*o."
It was the first and only word he'd said to me since reaching his place. The moment we walked through the doors of his townhome, I spilled my guts to him, trying to end things as quickly as possible so that I could retreat and do my best to never think about the entire situation again.

I stared back at him incredulously. I was sobbing. My face was red. My voice was shaking. I felt sick with every word. He was sitting back on the couch with his arms crossed, his jaw tight, looking totally unreadable.

"What do you mean "no"?"

"I mean no. I don't accept your breakup." He stood and threw his hands up in exasperation. "This is crazy, Kate. Things were fine just a few days ago."

I couldn't argue with that. I'd been doing such a fantastic job of ignoring my feelings about everything that I couldn't say one way or another whether things had been good. They certainly hadn't been bad, but did that necessarily mean they were good?

"Were they?"

He stared at me as if I'd just sprouted another head.

"Yes, Kate. Things were good. You were thinking about moving in with me. We saw each other almost every day. Your mother loves me."

"My mother doesn't know you."

He stopped storming around the room and crossed his arms as he glared at me.

"What the hell is that supposed to mean, Kate? That if she did know me, she wouldn't like me? Like you don't like me all of a sudden?"

"No, that's not what I meant at all. I just mean that the two of you have spent very little time together, is all. And I do like you. I just…" I hesitated, unsure if I should finish with the first thing that popped in my mind. It was thoughtless and hurtful, but deep down I knew it was true. "I don't want you."

Something flickered in his eyes, and he looked like he'd been punched in the gut. Tears welled up in my own eyes again. It wasn't fair for me to be so upset, but I hated hurting him.

"You don't mean that. There's never been anything that you've ever said or done that fits with that story."

"Dillon." I reached for his hand and pulled him down to the sofa. "Since the fire…I don't think I've stopped long enough to let myself think about what I want. Some things have happened recently that made me stop and reflect on everything, and I just don't believe that what we have is enough."

"What things?" The muscles in his jaw were bulging now. He was angry, and he didn't want me to see just how much.

"It doesn't matter."

He exploded off the couch and began pacing the room.

"For Christ's sake, Kate, you owe me more of an explanation than this. I was going to marry you. You were it for me. Babe…" He suddenly dropped to his knees and buried his head in my lap.

"I love you. You can't just end this and walk out like the last year didn't happen."

With a lump in my throat and tears streaming down my face, I pushed him away and stood. "I love you too, but I don't think either one of us loves the other like we should. There's no passion here; we're not crazy about each other."

He huffed and shook his head in dismissal. "Give me a break, Kate. Shit like that means nothing. This makes sense." He motioned between us. "We make sense."

He reached for me again, but I stepped away.

"I'm sorry, Dillon. The last thing I ever want to do is look back on my life and say *it made sense.* I want so much more than that."

My back was toward him as I reached the door, and he let out one low and angry chuckle.

"Good luck with that, Kate. Do you really think men will be knocking down your door now? Maybe a few years ago they would have, but not anymore. You're too damaged. You've got way more baggage than anybody's going to want to deal with."

I nearly dropped to the floor from the impact of his words. I'd known Dillon for years and never had he said anything so harsh to me. The one thing he knew would hurt me the most, the one worry I'd never spoken out loud, he'd vocalized. I could barely reconcile the fact that such cruel words had come from his mouth.

I wouldn't turn around and face him again. And I sure as hell wouldn't let him know how much his words had hurt me.

"Then I'd rather be alone."

I barely made it around the corner before I collapsed into the side of the nearest building and wept.

*T*hankfully, Mom still wasn't back by the time I made it to Laurel's apartment. I was able to lock myself inside my room and collect myself. It didn't take long. As hurtful as Dillon's words to me were, my therapist was right—I was a master at distraction. The fire had made that a necessity. When the pain got to be too much, or in truth, if any feeling got too strong, I could quickly tuck it away in some back corner of my mind where I didn't have to think about it by focusing on something outside myself.

I didn't have to look hard for something else to focus on either. Shortly after I closed the door to my room and gathered up Mr. Crinkles in my arm, my phone rang. I knew right away that it had to be Laurel from the lack of number on my phone.

"Hello?"

"Kate, it's me. Step into a room that Mom isn't in, okay?"

"No worries. Mom's not here. Oh my God, Laurel, it's so good to hear your voice!" I almost went straight into talking about all the research I'd done, but then I remembered Morna's directive that I not let Laurel know I'd spoken with her—which meant I shouldn't already know for certain that she was in the past. "You're okay? You're safe? Are you really...are you really in the past?" I could picture her leaning against some massive wooden door inside a creaky old castle. It made me tremble with excitement.

"Yes, yes, and yes. I'm okay. I'm safe. And I'm speaking to you from the year sixteen hundred and fifty-one."

I listened to her speak and peppered her with questions pertaining to the research I'd done. I was thrilled to hear that she was indeed at The Castle of Eight Lairds rather than at Conall Castle. While I'm sure Conall Castle was amazing, I'd devoted all of my research to the Isle and the strange legends surrounding it.

It was clear early on in our phone call that my sleepless nights of research had been well worth it. There were many things I knew more about than Laurel did. Laurel was, after all, living it. I was looking at it in retrospect. It was like being a fortune teller. Although, rather than telling someone else's future, I was looking into my own.

Laurel nearly croaked when I told her of my plan to go back with Mom and David. I heard the almost-reprimand in her voice when I confessed to being unable to really afford our plane tickets, but thankfully, she withheld her sisterly concern.

The more I talked, the more Laurel settled in. It gladdened me more than she could possibly know that I was able to be useful, even separated by so many centuries.

"The documentary told us about the legend, right—about The Eight and how they were bound to protect the Isle from the darkness that would threaten it if The Eight were ever broken? The book is much more specific. According to this text, the evil mentioned in the documentary is a faerie. While she may gain strength, she poses no real threat with just seven men."

I paused as Laurel interrupted. When she confirmed that the documentary was correct—that the evil on the Isle was indeed a faerie named Machara—I could've danced around the room in excitement. Not that I was excited that my sister was in such imminent danger, but I couldn't deny being excited to learn that such mystical creatures did indeed exist.

I went on to explain to Laurel that according to my research, six is the magic number. If The Eight lose two men without replacing one, the faerie bound by their magic would be able to break free from her prison.

"So, the book alludes to a prophecy given to Machara by her

father as punishment for something she'd done to anger him. It doesn't say what. He claimed that a time would come in Machara's life when she would be chained by the magic of men, but her life would end at the hands of mortal women."

It was nine mortal women to be exact, and I told Laurel this. Laurel's tone sounded worried any time she spoke. The more we talked, the more real everything seemed. This wasn't just a story. It was her life. It was my life. And if my sister's inclination to stay there was any indication, it was the life of the man she loved, as well.

"Okay, Kate, does it say anything about these women? Who are they?"

"That's where you come in, Laurel. You're one of them, and I'm pretty sure, so am I."

There was a brief moment of silence before Laurel responded. "Explain."

"Your name isn't mentioned specifically. It only refers to a Laird Allen's wife. It says that Laird Allen's wife is the first of the nine women who will ultimately destroy Machara, but that each woman will be tested in her own time and in her own way."

She asked the most obvious question next. "How do you know that you're one of them?"

"It wasn't even in the main text of the book. It doesn't go into detail about the nine women, but there was an author footnote at the bottom of one of the pages." I paused and almost stood to go and grab the book, but then decided against moving away from the door. I wanted to be able to block entry into the room. "I don't remember the exact wording, but it said something along the lines of: *Little is known of the women who lifted the castle's curse, though two of the nine were believed to be sisters, both blonde of hair and blue of eyes, though one had suffered much at the hands of a fire.*"

I sat patiently in the silence that followed as I allowed Laurel to process everything.

She agreed with what I already suspected—that Morna had added the footnote to give me a clue that I was supposed to go back, as well.

We chatted for some time, and I told her what I'd read of the druid who'd fallen in love with a fae and how he was said to have died as a result. Laurel said his name was Calder and that while he was not yet dead, she could see things ending in no other way for him.

"Laurel, I hope for your sake that Calder stays away. If he returns, I'm not sure there's much you'll be able to do to stop him from giving you to Machara."

Laurel's voice was small and frightened when she answered. "I know."

She was frightened. Before my conversation with Morna, I would've told her not to worry—that she had history on her side —but now, I was as scared as she was.

"Listen to me, Laurel. You can beat her if you're forced to face her. You're the smartest person I know. You're so much stronger than you think."

I heard her take a deep breath, and I wanted nothing more than to wrap her in a hug.

"Thank you, Kate. I need to go. I don't know if I'll be able to call for awhile. There's a lot I need to sort through here."

I nodded as if she could see me. "I know. I'll see you in a few weeks, okay?"

At that, Laurel spoke up. I could hear the smile in her tone. "About that. I can't believe I almost forgot. Listen, you don't have to look for Morna. I made a friend, another modern lady sent back in time by Morna. She lives at Cagair Castle, and they have their own portal. She says it's far easier to travel back through it than by Morna's magic. She told me that if I ever have anyone that needs to come through to send them there. She and her husband will escort you guys all the way to the Isle when you arrive."

"Are you serious?" I tried to feign surprise at her suggestion.

"Yes. Her name is Sydney. Just ask for her when you get there. I believe the other woman's name is Gillian. They will know what to do."

I could hear some shuffling from the other end of the phone, and I could sense that Laurel needed to go.

"Laurel, take care of yourself, okay?"

"I will. You too, Kate. I love you."

After relaying my own love for her, I hung up the phone, and curled up into a ball beneath my blankets in the hopes the warmth would stop me from shaking from both a wounded heart and fear for my sister.

CHAPTER 7

Sixteen Days Later

couldn't believe that out of everything I'd taken care of, out of every list I'd created and checked off, out of every possible scenario I'd thought through, that this was the one thing that hadn't crossed my mind. I was a smart woman. I didn't do stupid things. But my ignorance over this situation had me sobbing on the phone. I was heartbroken, and if I couldn't figure out a way around this, I was fairly certain there would be no putting me back together.

"What do you mean, there's not enough time? There has to be enough time. He's healthy. He's had all of his shots and check-ups. I've flown with him many times."

The travel agent kept her voice calm, but she gave me the same answer. "You've flown with him domestically, yes?"

My breath shook as I answered her. "Yes."

"I'm sorry, Ms. Adams, but international travel with animals is very different. Each country has its own rules. While you could've flown with your cat had you planned further in advance and had all of the correct documentation, I'm afraid there really is no way for us to get it this close to your trip. All of that has to be arranged way ahead of your actual departure date. I understand your sadness. I truly do."

"No." I was making a fool of myself, I knew, but I couldn't help it. I couldn't leave Mr. Crinkles behind. I wouldn't do it. "You really don't understand. I nearly died for him. I can't leave him here."

The woman sighed. "I don't mean to be cold, Ms. Adams, I really don't. Surely you can bear to be away from your cat for a few weeks. Don't you have friends who could watch him? If not, I know of some very good boarding facilities that I recommend to many of my clients when we plan their trips."

"I can't leave him with a friend, and I'd never board Mr. Crinkles."

I hung up the phone and sobbed into my pillow. I might have lost my arm saving Mr. Crinkles in the fire, but I'd never regretted it for a minute. If not for him, I would've died that night. He was the one who woke me as smoke filled my room.

If he couldn't go to Scotland, then neither could I.

---

*S*everal hours into my session of full-on pity, my phone rang. I knew from the blocked number that it was Laurel. I didn't even say hello to her as I answered. "Are you okay?"

"Yes."

She didn't sound okay. She sounded frightened and nervous. "What's going on?"

"Listen, Kate. I just wanted to tell you that everything is playing out as you said it would. Calder is back, and he is under Machara's control. The men have him bound right now, but I'm going to convince them to release him. This has to end. We can't keep Calder locked away, and I can't live with the fear of him taking me to her when he gets loose. I'd rather it be on my terms. I have a plan. Everything is going to be okay. But just in case it isn't, I wanted to call and tell you how much I love you."

I swallowed the lump in my throat. The last thing Laurel needed was to hear how upset I was at the possibility of losing her. I wanted to tell her that it was going to be okay, but I couldn't lie to her. I couldn't be certain that it would be.

"I love you too, Kate. Let me know the moment you've beaten that bitch, okay?"

She let out a small laugh, agreed to call me, and hung up the phone.

For months, I'd gone without tears, and now, for the second time in just as many weeks, I was left sobbing, but this time, I could see no distraction in sight.

CHAPTER 8

That night I had—like I often do—the strangest dream. I was in Scotland. Or, at least, I assumed I was in Scotland from the green, rolling landscape and the view of the ocean out on the horizon. I stood in the most beautiful clearing, with vibrant flowers surrounding me. What could only be described as a throne sat in the middle of a wide circle amongst the flowers. It was warm with no breeze, and I stood next to a tall man whose face was blurry to me. We approached the throne with trepidation, but suddenly I was pulled away from my traveling companion and tossed in front of the tall chair. When I glanced up, the seat was no longer empty. An otherworldly form of a man occupied the seat. My entire body felt alive in the strangest way. I looked down to see that my right arm was now whole, and I felt happier than I'd ever felt in my life. But just as quickly as I'd been placed before the throne, I was jerked away, tumbling backwards into an abyss. It made no sense, but it felt incredibly real.

The very next morning, I woke to the sound of the doorbell ringing. Expecting that Mom would answer it, I didn't move until the third ring. Eventually, I stood and stepped out into the living room, only to see a note from my mom taped to the door. *Gone to the gym. Be back soon. There's cereal out on the counter.*

I opened the door to find a nerdy-looking teenager bouncing back and forth from one foot to the other rather impatiently.

"Are you Kate Adams?"

I nodded without smiling. His chipper mood was pissing me off.

He extended a legal-sized envelope in my direction. "This is for you then." I watched as he glanced to my missing right arm. "Can you...can you sign?"

I reached out and jerked the envelope and the pen from his hand.

"I'm left-handed."

"Oh." His face lifted. "Well, that's lucky, ain't it?"

For the first time in days, I smiled. It was so much easier dealing with people who were frank about my injury than those who danced around it and stared at me awkwardly as if I couldn't see them.

"I suppose it is. Thank you for this. Hang on just a second."

Carrying the package inside, I grabbed some cash from my purse and gave him a tip before bidding him farewell.

As soon as I closed the door, I moved to open the envelope. Inside was a set of documents—everything I needed for Mr. Crinkles to be able to travel. There was also a small hard case and letter in the very bottom.

Dear Kate,

 Take a deep breath, dear. Surely you know I wouldn't let this stand. Of course, Mr. Crinkles must travel with you.

 As for your other worry, Laurel will call you soon, but she's fine. She ran her fiancé through with a sword, but he will heal in time, and

Machara is still locked away in her cell. So take one more deep breath, shake off that gloomy mood, and get ready for your new life in Scotland!

Remember what I told you, Kate. You had a reckless streak even before your accident. I'm afraid it may have grown even worse since losing your arm. There are many parts of our life where it serves us to be fearless: love, our passions, our work, but I've never been one who believed it wise to be fearless when it comes to our lives. I guess I treasure my own far too much for that. As far as I know, you only get one. I'd like to see you live a long one. So...while I don't know just how Machara will test you, just don't be a foolish idiot in how you respond to her.

I'll be watching from afar to see how things turn out for you.

With bated breath and love,
   Morna

P.S. I've spent a bit of time watching your mother as well, dear, and she's a little more high-strung than I imagined. And David—well he's a man of great intellect and will rage against his new reality. Inside the case is a small vial of something I cooked up for you. Whenever you decide to tell them about the time travel, put a few drops in their drinks. Don't worry, it won't affect their personalities at all, it will just make them accept the news a little more easily.

CHAPTER 9

The Isle of Eight Lairds—1651

"Paton said ye wished to see me?"

For the second time in a matter of weeks, Maddock stepped into Raudrich's bedchamber to visit with his injury-laden friend. The first set of injuries had been caused by the newest member of The Eight, Marcus, who'd broken his nose after finding him in bed with an unknowing Laurel. The second had come only days ago at the hand of his fiancée who'd run him straight through with a sword in order to save him from Machara.

Maddock neared Raudrich's bed as he shifted to prop himself up.

"Aye, I just wanted to tell ye that if ye ever listen to another one of Laurel's foolish orders again, I shall break both yer kneecaps."

Maddock laughed and crossed his arms casually over his chest.

"Ye do know that she saved us all, aye? If we hadna agreed to help her, she wouldna have been able to go through with her plan. And if she hadna gone through with her plan, she'd be dead, and ye'd be dead, and Machara would be free. Thus, we would all be dead."

"Do ye think ye could've used the word 'dead' any more times in that sentence, Maddock?"

He shook his head. "I doona think the point can be overemphasized. She saved our necks, Raudrich. Ye ought to be grateful for her."

Maddock watched as Raudrich grunted and ground his teeth.

"I am grateful to her, but I'm angry at every last one of ye for willingly putting her in danger."

He'd hated it at the time. He cared for Laurel immensely, but he'd seen sense in her plan, and he wasn't willing to apologize for his part in it.

"Aye, we know ye are angry. We've all heard the same from Marcus. 'Twas the right thing to do, and I'd do it again. Ye know that."

"Knock knock."

Maddock turned toward the sound of Laurel's voice in the doorway and smiled at her as she entered.

"Yer fiancé is daft if he thinks any of us regret doing as ye bid us to."

Laurel walked up next to him, winked at her soon-to-be husband, and answered him. "Yes, well. I don't regret it either."

"Not even stabbing me with a sword, lass?"

Maddock laughed as Laurel dismissed him with her hand.

"Not even that. Now, Maddock and I are going to leave you to rest. I need to speak with him about something."

Before Maddock could say anything else, Laurel latched onto his hand and began to pull him out into the hall.

Once the bedroom door was shut between them and Raudrich, she spoke. "Maddock, you know not only *where* I'm from but *when*, right?"

The Eight had known for years—ever since Raudrich's fast friendship with Sydney—that there were out-of-time lassies who often found themselves in Scotland at the hands of a witch none of them had ever met.

"Aye, I do. Why?"

"Well, I was hoping you might be willing to travel to Cagair and help escort my sister, my mother, and Marcus' dad back here. I trust you completely."

It pleased him to hear that he had Laurel's trust, and after his conversation with Harry, he was especially eager to meet Laurel's sister.

"O'course, I can. I'll leave at once."

Laurel raised one brow and crossed her arms in front of her chest. "You agreed to that too quickly. Why?"

He smiled mischievously. "If yer sister is half as pleasant as ye are, her presence will only bring more light to this castle."

She looked at him knowingly. "She's taken, Maddock."

"Married? Harry dinna tell me that."

Laurel looked surprised as she tilted her head gently to the side. "Harry? How does he know about Kate?"

"He only knows what Marcus told him."

"Ah." Laurel nodded, understanding. "Well, she's not married, but she's been dating the same man for several years now."

Maddock smiled, his hope resurfacing. "If she isna married, she isna taken. Besides, ye said nothing of this man coming back. I canna see how anyone can maintain a relationship with one of them living in our time and the other living hundreds of years in the future."

"Fair point. I guess with everything that's been going on, I'd not given much thought to what Kate might do about Dillon. But, you don't even know her. How can you be so sure that you'll like her so much?"

"I canna be sure, but if she's anything like ye, I shall like her verra much indeed."

Laurel smiled and leaned in to hug him. "Oh, Maddock, you're my favorite, too. Be careful, okay? And don't tell Paton what I said about the *favorite* thing since he's already agreed to go with you."

His smile disappeared at the realization that she'd not asked him first. "Favorite, ye say? Surely, if 'twas true, ye would've spoken to me before Paton."

"I only spoke to Paton first because I saw him first. I couldn't find you. So, listen. I really am sorry I have to ask you guys to do this anyway. Sydney had originally told me she and Callum would see them here, but she just received the happy news that she's pregnant, and I don't want her to travel that far while she's expecting. You do know the way to Cagair, don't you?"

He'd not traveled nearly as much as Raudrich, but his knowledge of Scotland was still wide.

"Aye, lass. I know where 'tis. Do ye mean for us to meet them in the Cagair of this time or theirs?"

Laurel shrugged. "That's up to you, really. Sydney and Callum will still be there and will help introduce them to everything, but if you'd like to go forward while you're there and see what it's like, I can't think of any reason why you shouldn't."

He definitely wanted to go forward.

oston—Two Days Later—Present Day

*J*ust as we were getting ready to head to the airport, Laurel called with a huge piece of news that she somehow neglected to tell me during our last phone call—she was engaged to Raudrich.

While I was genuinely thrilled for her, my own relationship status had me about ready to pull my hair out.

For days, Dillon had been trying to get ahold of me. For the last ten days, his name had popped up on my phone. Each time I sent it to voicemail.

"Don't you want to answer that? You were the one to end it, weren't you? What could he have done to cause you to be so cold to him?"

With all of our bags loaded in the car downstairs, there was just one thing left for me to do before we headed to the airport —doctor up the coffees I'd picked up with the potion Morna had sent with Mr. Crinkles' travel documents.

"I don't want to talk about it, Mom. It's over and nothing good would come from Dillon and me rehashing things. Here." I quickly swirled her coffee and extended it in her direction. "You carry this. I'll grab Mr. Crinkles. Let's get out of here."

With any luck, we'd arrive in Edinburgh with both Mom and David fully onboard with the concept of time travel.

CHAPTER 10

*E*dinburgh, Scotland

*D*espite Laurel's insistence that there were people at Cagair Castle who would welcome us whenever we decided to show up, I couldn't shake the feeling that it was very bad manners to just show up at someone's home unannounced. So, as Mom and David waited for our suitcases at baggage claim, I moved away to connect to the airport wi-fi so I could look up the number to call Cagair Castle.

A man's voice answered on the second ring. "'Ello."

"Hi...um..." I hesitated and my cheeks warmed as I realized I really should've planned what I was going to say before dialing. "This is going to seem like a very strange phone call. Do you mind if I ask who I'm speaking with?"

"Certainly, lass. My name is Orick. Might I ask ye the same question?"

"Yes, of course. My name is Kate. Is there...would it be possible for me to speak to either Sydney or Gillian?"

"I'm sorry, lass, but I'm afraid they've gone out for a bit." He paused, and I couldn't help but wonder if what he couldn't say was that they'd gone into the past using the castle's stairwell. "And they are unreachable at the moment. Are ye certain that I canna help ye?"

"Sure. Maybe. Do you know Morna?"

It seemed to me that was the most important question I could ask him. If he did know Morna, then surely he knew about the magic, and I could speak freely with him without sounding like a lunatic.

The man laughed, and his tone changed to one of recognition.

"Ah. I thought it strange that the phone was ringing. Rarely happens. Ye must be Laurel's sister, aye? Sydney told us to be expecting ye. Come on then. The lassies should be back by evening. If they are not, I'll see that rooms are ready for ye. How many others are with ye?"

I let out a big sigh of relief.

"Oh, thank you so, so much. Just me and two others."

"Perfect. I'll see that three spare rooms are ready for this evening. Safe travels. We shall see ye soon."

He hung up before I could say goodbye. By the time I turned around, my mother was standing right next to me, her hand inside Mr. Crinkles' carrier to pet him. She glanced at the phone and then back at me, and her cheeks flushed with excitement.

"Was that Dillon? Did you finally give in and answer the phone?"

I sighed and shook my head. Morna's potion had worked wonderfully. It had been way too easy to tell them everything on the plane. They listened quietly, took a minute to collect themselves, and then somehow—obviously due to the magic—were able to come to the conclusion that everything I said made sense. They both had no desire to be separated from their children, so they were as ready to go into the past as I was. Unfortunately, the potion seemed to have no effect on my mother's desire to meddle in my love life.

"No, it wasn't Dillon. I called Cagair Castle just to let them know that we were on our way there. I'm not going to be speaking to Dillon again. Please let it go."

She pinched her lips together and furrowed her brows. "Okay, dear, I just really think it would be best if you spoke to him. It's possible he really needs to get ahold of you."

Ignoring her, I threw my head to the side to motion toward the rental car building and walked on ahead.

"Let's get going. I'm eager to get there."

agair Castle

a t the advice of Sydney and Gillian—both of whom were beautiful, kind, and had husbands that looked like male models—we agreed to wait until after dinner to be shown to our rooms. They both believed that if we saw them now, we'd be too tempted to rest, and the best thing we could do to adjust to the time change would be to power through the rest of the day.

Instead, we spent a lovely day at the castle exploring the grounds with the owners and having a lovely dinner filled with great conversation.

Once dinner was over, and it was deemed late enough for us to go to sleep, Gillian led us to our rooms.

David looked awestruck as he stared down the hallway lined with doors. He was such an enjoyable travel companion. He was so gleeful about everything. "There are so many rooms. How do you not forget which one is yours?"

"Well, all of our rooms are in another wing that has fewer rooms, so that makes it a little easier. This room is yours, David. There are extra pillows and blankets in the wardrobe, and there are towels in the cabinet in the bathroom. If you need anything else, I'll hang around in the sitting room for awhile to make sure that you guys are settled."

He nodded, thanked her, and opened the door to the room. Before stepping inside, he turned to ask one last question. "What are the other room assignments?"

I felt my brows lift at his question. Why did he need to know which rooms we were staying in? I looked over at Gillian to see that her confused expression matched my own.

Before she could respond, David attempted to course correct. "You know, just in case there's some emergency and I need to rescue them. If I had to open every door, I might not make it in time."

I smiled at him and leaned in to give him a hug goodnight. "You would rescue us, wouldn't you, David?"

He squeezed me tightly before pulling away. "Of course I would. Now which room is whose?"

"Myla is in the third room from the stairwell on the other side of the hall, and Kate is closest to the stairwell on the other side."

David smiled and gave a quick nod before disappearing into his room.

Gillian moved to loop her right arm with my left as she walked me over to the room they'd set aside for me.

"They're both as lovely as you are. All right, here is your room. The rooms are set up in much the same way so you can find pillows and towels in the same places I told David. The only difference between this room and the others is that it shares a connecting bathroom with the room next to it, but don't worry, it's unoccupied. Since your escorts have yet to arrive, I suspect they won't get here until morning."

"Escorts?" I was under the impression that Sydney and her husband would be seeing us to the Isle.

"Oh." Gillian shook her head as if she just remembered. "We all thought you knew. Sydney found out she was pregnant a few weeks ago and doesn't feel comfortable traveling that far in such cool weather. Your sister is sending Maddock and Paton—two of the other men on the Isle—to see you guys back."

"That's wonderful!" I smiled at such happy news for Sydney. I would have to remember to congratulate her in the morning.

Gillian nodded in agreement. "Yes, it is. We are all very excited. Anyway, please do make yourself at home. I don't want you to feel as if you have to stay cooped up in your room all night. Feel free to roam around the castle or the grounds. The moon is bright tonight. You should be able to see just fine, and the garden out back is lit anyway. Do you need anything?"

I shook my head. "No. Thank you so much for all of this."

I was so sleepy I was certain I would fall asleep the moment my head hit the pillow. Instead, the moment I lay down, my mind started racing a million miles a minute.

Mom's obsession with Dillon's phone calls to me didn't make sense, and now that I had a moment to myself, they were starting to worry me. A lot. Something was amiss about the entire situation. Come morning, I was intent on finding out exactly what it was.

"*Y*ou two look exhausted."

The journey from The Isle to Cagair Castle had been a miserable one. He and Paton rode hard, but with the rain and the mud, the journey had been slower than expected. When they rode up to the front door of the castle, they were beyond weary.

"Aye, 'twas wretched weather the whole way. Thank ye for waiting up for us."

Sydney waved a dismissive hand as Callum came outside and gathered their horses.

"It was no trouble at all. Callum will see your horses to the stables. I'd originally planned for you to sleep in this century tonight, but both of you really look like you could use a nice hot shower. Wanna sleep in the twenty-first century?"

He wasn't sure what a shower was, but anything described as *nice* and *hot* sounded too good to pass up.

"Every muscle in my body aches, and I doona know if I will ever be able to get warm again, so if ye think there is something in yer own time that can help us with that, I'll sleep anywhere ye wish."

Sydney laughed.

"You'll love it. Let's go."

or hours I lay in the massive, perfectly soft bed with my eyes wide open and my mind churning with worry. Why had my mother been so insistent that I answer Dillon's phone calls? It wasn't unusual for her to be pushy about things—especially the love lives of her daughters—but in this case, it didn't make a lot of sense to me. She *didn't* know Dillon that well. I met him long after she'd moved to Florida, and she'd only met him on her visits to Boston and for brief times during the first few months after the fire when she was there to care for me around the clock. She'd had way closer relationships with past boyfriends of mine. Why the sudden strong attachment to Dillon?

Had he called her and made her feel sorry for him? Had he somehow convinced her to try to plead his case to me? If so, he obviously hadn't told her what he'd said to me. If my mother had heard that, she'd have driven across town to kick his ass herself, I was certain.

Mr. Crinkles meowed at the end of the bed and the sound reminded me to breathe. Crink, as I lovingly sometimes referred to him, was so good at picking up on my energy. He could tell when I was worked up. As I forced myself to take a deep breath, I realized how pointless my worries were. I was in Scotland. This time tomorrow, there would be hundreds of years between me and Dillon. So what if he'd called my mother? He was in the States, and I was here, and I soon wouldn't have a phone for him to call.

"Thank you." I sat up in the bed and leaned down to give Mr. Crinkles a quick snuggle as my worry slowly drifted away.

As my unnecessary panic came to an end, I was able to relax enough for my jet lag induced exhaustion to catch up with me, and it didn't take long for my eyes to begin to close as I drifted off to sleep. Just as I reached the cusp of full-on unconsciousness, a sudden clanging began in the bathroom attached to my room, followed shortly by what I could only assume was Gaelic cursing.

Our escorts had arrived.

I waited for a moment before turning on the lights in the hopes that whatever trouble the man was having would end, but the unusual sounds only continued. Eventually, I decided that if I didn't go to help him, he would wake up the whole castle.

Reaching over to the small lamp on the nightstand, I flipped on the switch and walked over to the door before attempting to address the man inside.

Knocking gently, I spoke to him. "Do you need some help?"

The clamoring stopped and a deep, accented, ridiculously sexy voice answered me. "Aye. I'd be much obliged if ye would show me how to work this, this..." He hesitated as if he were trying to remember the word *shower*.

As he finished, I heard his hand reach for the knob. I looked up at him as he came into view, and the light from the bathroom spilled into my own barely-lit room.

He was a good foot taller than me, and while he was lean, he had broad shoulders that showed how strong he was and made him look especially masculine. His hair was short, but had a little bit of length on top and I couldn't help but think that the style of his hair was remarkably modern. Except for the filthy linen shirt and kilt, he didn't look that out of place in this time.

I scanned him for longer than was probably appropriate before I actually looked up at his face. When I finally did, he was smiling. The beauty of him caused my breath to catch in my chest on an almost auditory level.

With most of his body now in the shadow of the doorway, I couldn't quite make out the color of his eyes, but his smile was wide and bright and his nose, while larger in the middle from what I assumed was a past break, was endearing. It made what would've been an intimidatingly handsome face just a little more approachable. He even had a smattering of freckles on both cheeks that I could just make out in the semi-darkness that allowed me to immediately picture what he must've looked like as a boy.

"Ye must be Kate, lass. Ye and yer sister resemble one another greatly."

Taking in an embarrassingly shaky breath, I nodded as I tried to act like the grown woman I was. "Yes, I'm Kate. You're..." I paused as I scanned through the portrait I'd seen of The Eight during my research. "Maddock?"

He grinned again and something in my stomach turned over. "Aye. How did ye know that?"

"I've read quite a lot about you. I did some research once I knew Laurel was there. In one of the books, there's a portrait of all of you, and your names were below."

"Ah."

There was a brief moment of awkward silence and my mind

starting screaming at me to just do something. I reacted by thrusting out my left hand so he could shake it.

"It's nice to meet you, Maddock."

He turned his head as he looked down at my hand and chuckled softly. "Ye too, Kate." Taking my hand, he raised it to his lips and gently brushed them against my knuckles. My stomach clenched and I grew hot all over.

"Um...how about I get this shower started for you?"

"Please, lass. I canna wait to see how it works."

He stepped aside so I could enter the bathroom, and my shoulder brushed against his chest as I passed him.

"Did Sydney not offer to help you? I'm surprised."

I could feel the heat of him as he turned and took a step toward me.

"Ach, she did, but the lass was verra tired from waiting up for us, and Paton needed her help as well, so I told her I could manage on my own. I never dreamed 'twould be so difficult to manage."

I turned and looked around the bathroom to see if he'd laid any clothes out. I imagined he hadn't. "Do you have anything else to wear after you get out of the shower?"

He scrunched up his nose. "I dinna think of it. No, lass, I doona have a thing."

I gently touched the side of his arm to scoot him over so I could get to the cabinet behind him. "Well, those are too dirty to put back on. I think I saw a robe in here that should fit you. There are towels, too."

He didn't say anything, and I could see by his expression that he was just watching to see what I meant by all of that.

I grabbed the towel and twisted my arm behind me to hand it to him.

"To dry off with. You can hang it on the hook beside the shower."

When he took it from my hand, I reached for the robe and shook it out before me. It was plenty big for him.

"And you can put this on afterwards if you want something to sleep in."

He laughed as he took the robe from my hand. "I doona sleep in anything, lass. Not unless I'm outdoors. Even then, I prefer to do so only if 'tis so cold I canna stand it."

Images of what he might look like naked flashed through my mind, and I quickly stepped around him again to reach into the bathtub-shower combo.

"You were probably closer to getting this to work than you think. You have to turn on both knobs and adjust them until it gets to the temperature you want."

"The hot water comes right away?" His voice sounded astounded.

I turned on the water and let it warm. "Pretty quickly, yes. How hot would you like it?"

"Hot, lass. I doona know if I've ever been so excited before."

I smiled as the water began to run hot and I turned around and slammed my face right into his chest. I'd not realized that he'd leaned in so close to watch what I was doing.

"Oh, I'm sorry."

He reached up to grip both my arms as he steadied me. "No need to apologize, lass. I should've said I was behind ye. I wanted to see how ye worked the water."

"Why don't you feel that and see if it's warm enough for you? If it's too hot, let me know, and I'll cool it down a bit."

He didn't give me time to move out of the way before he leaned in and reached around me.

Our faces were inches from each other, and I smiled as his eyes widened as he placed his hand beneath the faucet.

"'Tis perfect."

"Good. You see that little knob sticking up above the faucet?"

He nodded.

"Pull that up, and the water will come out of that head at the top."

He did as I instructed and let out a gasp as the water began to fall behind my back.

"I may stay beneath it all night."

I laughed and reluctantly scooted to the side to step away from him. "I'll leave you to it then."

I made it to the door when he called back to me. "Kate?"

I twisted and had to suppress my own gasp of delight. In the seconds it had taken me to walk toward my bedroom, he'd removed his shirt in his haste to get into the shower. He was every bit as perfect looking as I'd imagined him. Every muscle strong and sculpted.

"Yes?"

"Thank ye."

I smiled and swallowed the needy lump that had suddenly risen in my throat.

"You're welcome. Enjoy that. I'll see you in the morning."

I cast my eyes to the ceiling as I walked into my room and closed the bathroom door between us.

Shit. This man was trouble. Trouble that was already making me feel way more than I was comfortable with.

CHAPTER 12

hank Brighid for his kilt. The thick fabric was all that had hidden his excitement from Kate's view. The moment she'd turned into him, bumping against his chest, the smell of her, fresh and flowery, had wafted up toward his nose, making him yearn for her. It had been all he could do not to pull her against him right there and press his mouth to hers.

God, she was beautiful. He'd never doubted she would be pretty, but she was more stunning than he had imagined. She was shorter and more petite than her sister, and her hair was even more blonde than Laurel's. Her hair had been pulled up messily into a knot on the top of her head, and he couldn't help but wonder just how long it would drop down her back if he pulled it from its hold.

Her night clothes were unlike any he'd ever seen before. She wore breaches that went up between her thighs, and the thin, shiny fabric was so short he could see every last bit of her legs. And the top—ach, the top—it clung to her, emphasizing the fullness of her breasts. Her nipples had been hard beneath the fabric, as clear to him as his hardness would've been to her if not for the saving grace of his kilt.

It took a moment for him to collect himself after she closed the door separating them. As he unpinned his kilt and allowed it to drop to the floor, he couldn't resist the urge to press his hand to himself to relieve the pressure of his wanting.

His breath shaky from both his sudden need of the woman he'd just met and his excitement from the impending shower, he stepped beneath the hot spray and groaned.

It felt so good. The pressure beat against his back; the heat melted the knots in his muscles. Dirt ran off him, discoloring the water dripping off his body.

He turned toward the spray, reveling in the feeling of it pounding against his trail-weathered cheeks. He sighed and closed his eyes. As images of Kate in her scandalous night clothes danced beneath his lids, he reached one hand down beneath the warm spray to remedy what she'd done to him.

*fter leaving Maddock to shower, once again, I couldn't sleep. Visions of him running his soapy hands up and down his body, smiling as he enjoyed the sensation of spraying water for the first time, flooded my mind. It made me hot and horny, and I sincerely wanted nothing more than to join him in that shower.

It was a ridiculous thought, but I allowed myself to enjoy the fantasy guilt-free. Any straight woman under the age of ninety—possibly even past that—would've had the same thoughts after seeing that man bare chested.

When the sound of the shower stopped, I listened to him rummage around the bathroom, smiling as I pictured him exploring and oohing and aahing at all of the surprising things he'd never seen before.

I hit my head on the headboard when there was a sudden soft knock on the door between us.

I all but jumped from the bed as I rushed toward the door. When I reached it, I placed my mouth up against it so he could hear me.

"Do you need some more help?"

He opened the door quickly, and I almost fell into him again but recovered and righted myself as I stumbled away from him.

"No, lass. 'Tis only..." He paused and pointed toward the lamp on the nightstand. "I could see the light from beneath the door and I wondered if ye were still awake. I doona think I can sleep. If ye canna as well, I thought we could keep each other company."

He shrugged inside the plush robe he was wrapped in as if he was slightly self-conscious that I would turn him away.

I smiled. "Sure. Come on in. You can tell me all about what my sister's been up to since she arrived there. I've haven't been able to talk to her nearly as much as I would like to."

His shoulders relaxed as he stepped into the room. Mr. Crinkles stood up on the bed and watched him carefully. Maddock saw him right away, and when his first reaction was to smile at the sight of my beloved companion, I immediately liked him a little bit more.

"Is the creature a he or a she, lass?"

I moved to the bed to pick him up before carrying him over to Maddock so they could meet one another.

"A he. Maddock, meet Mr. Crinkles." I looked down at Crink. "Mr. Crinkles, meet Maddock."

Hesitantly, Maddock reached for him, and I handed him over. If Mr. Crinkles didn't like him, he'd let it be known quickly.

Luckily, Maddock was covered in terry cloth from his neck down to the mid-length of his calf so Mr. Crinkles couldn't do too much damage if he decided to swat at him.

Crink melted into Maddock's arms and began to purr much like he'd done with Morna.

"Did you spell him or something? He had the same reaction with the witch, Morna."

Maddock smiled and rubbed the top of Mr. Crinkles' head. "No, lass, I wouldna dare, but I'm not surprised that he's taken to me. All animals are sensitive to magic, cats more so than many. He can sense it, and in some way feels connected to it."

It didn't surprise me to hear it. Mr. Crinkles had always seemed a little magical to me. He had, after all, saved my life that night so many months ago.

Content that my cat wasn't going to scratch Maddock's eyes out, I looked around the room for a place for us to settle in. It was a very large room, but aside from the bed, there was only one other place to sit—a large chair in the far corner of the room. It looked like it weighed about eight hundred pounds.

"Why don't you bring him back over to the bed? We can sit there and visit."

He raised his brows in surprise. "Ye are inviting me to yer bed, lass?"

I chuckled nervously—God how I wanted to—as I turned my back toward him and walked over to the bed. I crawled up onto the mattress, propped up the pillows against the headboard and sat down cross-legged on top of the covers.

"I'm inviting you to sit *on top* of my bed."

He winked at me and set Mr. Crinkles down on the bed. "I jest, lass. Can I ask ye something?"

I shrugged. "Of course, but only if you sit down."

He hesitated then sat down on the edge and leaned over to lay across the bed and rested his face into the palm of his hand.

"If I sit as ye are, ye might see enough of me to give ye nightmares."

I laughed and swallowed the words that first came to my mind: *Or wet dreams.*

"Okay, what's your question?"

"Why would ye want to leave here? Why would anyone want to leave this time? Ye have pleasures and wonders here I couldna dream of, and all I've truly seen is the shower."

"When your need for a fresh start outweighs your need for convenience, it's an easy decision to make."

The honest confession slipped out before I could stop it, and I immediately tensed after spilling the words. They were the truth, but they made it clear I wasn't happy here, and I never liked anyone to know that I wasn't truly happy.

I could tell by Maddock's guarded gaze that he'd noticed my face shift. Whether it was out of politeness or disinterest, he didn't press me further, and for that, I was grateful.

"Now, let me ask you a question. Is he good enough for my sister? Laurel called me yesterday to tell me she and Raudrich were engaged."

His brows pinched together in confusion. "She *called* ye?"

"It doesn't matter. Is he?"

He shook his head without hesitation. "No, but he loves her verra much. And in fairness, I couldna love yer sister more if she were my own kin, so I doona know if I would ever think anyone was good enough for her."

"I agree. No one is."

"What of ye, Kate? Yer sister mentioned that ye've a love of yer own. Is he sleeping in another room, or did ye leave him behind for this new life of yers?"

Had it been any other circumstance, or perhaps with any other person, I would've squirmed away from the topic of Dillon. After spending so many hours spinning out about him earlier, he wasn't really a topic I wanted to discuss. But he was, even if I didn't want to admit it, still on my mind, and for some reason, none of my normal defense mechanisms rose up at Maddock's question.

I couldn't tell if it was something about his presence that calmed me or if I was just simply too exhausted to put up my usual defenses—perhaps I was jet lag drunk. Whatever it was, it felt nice to speak honestly without my words causing me some sort of physical or emotional pain, so I did so freely.

"I ended things with him a few weeks ago. He won't be coming with us."

His lips pulled to the side in a sympathetic expression as he spoke. "Ye must be grieving for him. 'Tis never easy to say goodbye to those we care for, even if we know 'tis right for us to do so."

"Perhaps I should be grieving, but it was never right between us."

"Did ye love him?"

I waited a moment before answering. I wanted to be sure that my first reaction was truly how I felt. "I thought I did. I do love him in the sense that I care about him. I would never want anything bad to happen to him. I hope he's happy, but I don't think that I was in love with him. I don't miss him, and I don't believe I ever shall."

"Then you werena in love with him, lass."

I nodded in agreement. "Right? I mean, I just believe it should be more intense between two people than it was with Dillon and me. I want that jolt to run through me every time I look at the person I'm with; I want to light up when I'm in a room and he glances my way; I want..." I paused to see him watching me closely, and warmth spread through my whole body. It was an intimate, knowing glance, and something silent passed between us that made me wonder if perhaps his reaction to me wasn't so different from mine to him. "I just want more."

He shook his head to relieve the intensity between us. "Ye deserve more, lass. Do ye mind..." He pointed to my missing right arm. "Does it pain ye to speak of the fire?"

Usually, it did, but I didn't feel like it would be so painful to talk about it with him.

"Sometimes, but my therapist would tell me that speaking about it will only make it easier for me to move on."

He said nothing, giving me plenty of time to talk through it at my own pace.

"It was a normal night. I worked a little later than usual. I was over at a client's house finishing up a decorating job. I came home thrilled that the client had loved the new bathroom I'd designed for her, but I was also exhausted.

"I've always been a very heavy sleeper. I'm hard to wake, and when I'm tired, I sleep like the dead. Anyway, the fire started in the apartment above me. The old man that lived there left his stove on and something caught, and the entire building went up so quickly. The alarms sounded, and most people woke up and were able to evacuate, but I slept right through it.

"By the time Mr. Crinkles managed to wake me, the apartment was filled with smoke. We nearly made it out before part of the ceiling caved in and pinned us both to the ground. Debris flew into Mr. Crinkles' eye causing him to lose it, and my arm got pinned beneath the ceiling. It's a miracle that firefighters were able to pull us both out and that all we lost were an eye and an arm."

BETHANY CLAIRE

He shook his head and his gaze looked sad. "I canna imagine how frightened ye were. How great the pain must have been."

"In all honesty, I wasn't frightened. It happened too quickly for me to be scared, and the pain was nothing then." I shuddered thinking about the weeks and months of recovery afterward. "That came later. Luckily, I didn't have too many burns on my body. That was the one blessing about the way things fell. The part of the building that landed on me and Crink didn't actually catch on fire, so we were shielded from most of the flames.

"You asked before why anyone would want to leave here. Visiting with you has driven home my reason even more. My roots are too deep in Boston. Every place I go—my work, Laurel's apartment building, all of my favorite restaurants—everyone knows me. Or at least they did know me. Now, they look at me as if I went somewhere in that fire. They don't look at me the same because they know who I was before. I changed. I know that, but I didn't die. I'm still here, but I'm not sure everyone else knows that. All you can see is who I am now, and that's more refreshing than I know how to express. I'm ready to leave everything behind. I don't think I ever could've really healed there."

He leaned forward with his hand that wasn't holding up his head and gave my knee a gentle squeeze. "I thought yer sister was the bravest lass I knew. I doona know if I can say that anymore."

I laughed and rolled my eyes. "Brave is the very last thing I am. I'm scared of everything."

"O'course ye are. We are all scared, but most of us allow that fear to keep us from doing things. Ye doona do that."

We spent the rest of the night talking. We spoke of the other men on the Isle and of Laurel's throwdown with Machara. We spoke of serious things and silly things. By the time the sun

82

began to peek through the windows, I was certain I'd never been so happy to start a day on so little sleep.

"I think ye should go and speak to yer mother about what is troubling ye now, lass. Before the castle wakes and the day truly begins. The time just before ye sleep and just after ye wake hold a special sort of magic. People are more prone to honesty; to bearing their soul, if ye will."

At some point in the night, we'd circled back around to the topic of Dillon, and I'd mentioned my worry over my mother's insistence that I speak with him. He was right, I wanted to find out what was up.

Standing and stretching from hours of sitting there on the bed, I smiled at him. "You sound as if you know this from experience."

He motioned between the two of us. "Look at us, lass. We hardly know one another and yet we met each other during that magical time of day I just mentioned, and we spent the whole night speaking to one another like old friends."

Or lovers. I kept that thought to myself.

"You're right. I'll go talk to her now."

---

*S*tepping out into the hallway, I could see that the light in Mom's bedroom was already on as I'd suspected it would be. She enjoyed rising early.

It never occurred to me to knock before entering. I turned the knob and flung it open without a second thought.

The only way for me to make sense of my ridiculously delayed reaction is to chalk it up to shock. Every fiber in my being had known precisely what I would see when stepping inside my mother's room. I would find her propped up in bed, reading glasses on and a book in her hands, enjoying the quiet minutes before everyone else was awake.

My brain simply didn't know how to comprehend what I was seeing.

Mom was propped up in the bed, but she wore no reading glasses, and there wasn't a book in sight. Instead, she was naked, and her breasts greeted me as I stared at her in confusion.

"Mom? Did you sleep nude?"

It should've been so obvious to me, but I just wasn't getting it.

Her panicked voice was immediate. "Kate! You don't just go around opening doors without knocking."

I snorted, still astonishingly slow on the uptake. "Seriously? You're one to talk. Do you even know how to knock? I mean..."

There was the briefest of shuffling noises, and for the first time since stepping inside the room, I glanced toward her bathroom.

David stood totally naked in the doorway, both palms spread wide to cover up his junk.

He and I must've stared at each other for a solid five seconds of horror. Eventually, as my mouth still hung wide open from shock, he spoke. "Good morning, Kate. I guess the cat's out of the bag."

CHAPTER 13

J stood there for way too long as my eyes darted back and forth between David in the bathroom doorway and my mother in the bed. I wouldn't have been any more shocked if I'd walked in on Mom in bed with George Clooney.

"I...uh...excuse me." Reaching for the knob, I pulled the door shut and backed away from the scene slowly.

It was as if all of my muscles slowed down, making the walk down the hallway and down the stairs slow and heavy.

I could hear Maddock call after me as I moved away from the scene, but I kept walking until I reached the castle's main floor and turned down the staircase leading to the castle's kitchens. All I could think was that I needed coffee. Now. It was the only thing that might help my brain recover from the trauma it had experienced.

"Kate, lass, are ye all right?"

Maddock was just a few steps behind me, and I shook my head no as I walked into the kitchen.

"I just walked in on my mother and David naked together. I'm not sure if I'll be all right ever again."

Appearing out of the cupboard to the right of the kitchen, Sydney gasped as she looked at my ashen expression and then laughed softly.

"Eeek. Yeah, it doesn't get much worse than that, does it?" She studied my expression a moment longer before adding. "Wait. Did you not know they were together?"

I shook my head as Maddock appeared beside me in my peripheral vision.

"Did *you* know?"

Sydney gave me a sympathetic nod as she reached behind me to flip on the coffee maker as if she'd read my mind. "Honestly, I assumed they were. He touched her arm at least five times over dinner last night. And the knowing glances that seemed to pass between the two of them were frequent."

So many little instances flashed through my mind. Mom's early morning trips to the gym, her reaction when I'd mentioned eating dinner with David, her offer to call him about said dinner, and even her reaction *at* the dinner should've clued me in, but it obviously never crossed my mind.

Shrugging as acceptance washed through me, I smiled for the first time since opening that bedroom door. "Actually...I guess it makes sense, but I really didn't have a clue."

"Ye look as if ye might be cold, lass." Maddock spoke for the first time since we'd entered the kitchen and surprised me by moving to my back, where he reached up and placed both hands on either side of my arms as he gently rubbed them up and down to warm me.

Normally, I was touchy about letting people near the site of the amputation, mostly because everyone always acted so weird about it, but Maddock didn't hesitate as he ran his palm all the way down to where my arm now ended at the elbow. The fact that he didn't hesitate made it impossible for me to feel self-conscious about it. It felt nice, and as the chill in my body subsided, I took a deep breath and relaxed into him.

Sydney clenched her teeth nervously as she watched me. I immediately grew tense again.

"Don't relax too much just yet. I'm afraid something else happened this morning that is bound to be a shock."

Maddock's hands stilled on my shoulders at Sydney's words.

I stepped away from him so I could steady myself on the island countertop.

"What is it? What happened?"

"More like *who* happened, really. I woke this morning and—as I do every morning—made my way through the magical stairwell that connects the Cagair of this time to the Cagair of the seventeenth century so that I could cook breakfast. When I came out of the stairwell and made my way around to the front door of the castle, there was a car running outside. As I approached, a man exited and came over to greet me. He said his name was Dillon. He claims to be your boyfriend."

CHAPTER 14

*E*very bit of my worrying had been justified. I had no doubt that somehow my mother was involved with Dillon's arrival here at the castle. She had to be. Otherwise, I could think of no way for him to know where we were.

I shook my head as I braced my arm on the countertop and bent to shield my face and head into the crook of my arm as I groaned. "I'm going to kill her."

"Who?" Sydney's voice sounded confused.

"My mother. She helped him do this. She helped him find me. That's why she was so insistent that I answer his calls." I glanced up from my bent position to see her staring down at me with sympathy.

"I can make him leave if you'd like."

I shook my head before turning back to the covered safety of my arm. "No, I'm going to have to deal with this. Where is he?"

There was the sudden sound of several sets of footsteps on the floor above, and it sounded to me as if they were approaching the stairwell.

"I bet that's him. Callum was giving him a tour of the castle. I think they are headed down here now."

I made a dramatic sound of dread, as if I were crying, but stopped the moment I felt Maddock's hands lift me from the island.

He spun me toward him, keeping his grip tight on my shoulders as his eyes stared into my own.

"Do ye want him here, lass?"

I shook my head no.

"From what ye've said of him, I doona think him a man that understands anything easily with words alone. Mayhap, ye should give him something else to let him know ye are through with him."

I shrugged beneath Maddock's grip. "Oh yeah? What would that be?"

Mischief flashed in his green eyes, and my body lit up all over. "Do ye trust me?"

I thought of all the rarely spoken things I'd trusted him with last night. I thought of my sister's love for him and her obvious trust in sending him here to see us to the Isle safely. Even if he was still a stranger, I knew my answer.

"Yes."

He smiled as his left hand released its grip on my shoulders and smoothly slid down to my lower back where he pulled me close against him.

I could hear Dillon descending the stairs to the kitchen, but I kept my eyes locked with Maddock's.

The moment Dillon stepped into the room and could easily see the two of us pressed against one another, Maddock bent his head and kissed me.

here was no warm-up to his kiss. No light touch of his lips to see if I would accept them, no delicate trail along my jaw. Immediately, his lips were hot and urgent against my own. At first, I stiffened in response, my back going rigid in shock, but it only took a moment before my body became liquid against him, my mind surrendering to the pleasure of his lips dancing against my own.

As Maddock's tongue flickered into my mouth—a testing, teasing gesture that invited me to play with him—I responded in kind.

He kissed me for longer than was necessary—I heard Dillon turn around and head back up the stairs shortly after he saw the two of us—but I made no effort to pull away. My body was too alive, my mind too sludgy to do anything other than surrender to how good it felt to kiss him.

He was lost in it, too. He held me so close against him, I could feel the need balled up tight throughout every muscle in his body. His breath was shaky and rough, his lips heavy and urgent. It was only once his hands began to roam up and down my body that he seemed to remember what he was doing and why. When he finally did pull away, he looked as swept up as I felt.

He glanced around the room uncomfortably. "I...." He let out a shaky breath and gave me a gentle smile. "I think it worked, lass. He's gone. Best ye go to him. Tell him whatever will make him see that ye meant every word ye said to him before. If ye need to use me, I'll go along with whatever ye tell him."

If not for the support of the kitchen island behind me, I would've fallen over when he stepped away. I turned to my right to see Sydney gaping at us with her mouth and eyes wide open.

Unsure of what to say to any of them, I simply nodded in acknowledgment of Maddock's suggestion and awkwardly scooted past a perplexed-looking Callum on the stairs as I made my way up to find Dillon.

I didn't have to look far. He was sitting on the grand entrance stairway, with his face in his hands as I approached.

He glanced up and looked at me with weary eyes. "Is he the reason you ended things?" He lifted his head and pointed toward the kitchen. "Is that why you came to Scotland?"

"What?" I shook my head as I moved to sit next to him. "Of course it's not. Do you really think I'd cheat on you?"

He sighed and shifted so that he faced me. "No, I don't. How long have you known him?"

I glanced over at the grandfather clock near the entryway. "All of nine hours."

He shook his head in disbelief. "I guess I deserve this." He reached out to grab my hand as tears filled his eyes. "I'm so, so sorry, Kate. I haven't been able to eat, haven't been able to sleep since you left my place that night. You have to know...I didn't mean it. What I said..."

He paused and let out a loud sob that startled me so much I jumped. I'd never seen him cry before.

He bent until his head was all the way in my lap, and he cried as he spoke. "I truly didn't mean it. Please, Kate. Please forgive me. I can't live with myself knowing I said something so cruel to you. Knowing that you think I truly believe that. Of course, he wants you. God, any man with half a brain cell would want you. I was just hurt, Kate. Really, really hurt."

I believed him. Even though his words hurt me so much in that moment, none of them had sounded like him. And there was no way this apology was disingenuous.

Giving him a gentle push with my hand, I waited until he raised his head from my lap. "I know that, Dillon. I forgive you. But it doesn't change anything."

He nodded sadly. "I know."

I dropped my hand and tilted my head in confusion. "Then what are you doing here? Why come all this way?"

He smiled for the first time. "Well, I couldn't really tell you how sorry I was, could I? You would never answer your phone. I'll admit that when your mother first called me, I thought maybe I had a chance. She seemed to think I did, but after several weeks of my calls being sent to your voicemail, I knew my chances were slim. I still needed to say I was sorry."

Once again, my tendency to avoid had caused problems. If only I'd answered the phone, I could've heard his apology and kept him from flying halfway across the world.

"I'm sorry I made you come all the way here to tell me that."

He shook his head and stood, offering me his hand so he could help pull me up. "I'm not."

"Really? Why not?"

"I didn't like seeing you kissing another man. I can't deny

93

that, but watching that kiss made me realize something—you never, not once, kissed me the way you kissed him."

I jerked uncomfortably as I looked up at him. "I didn't kiss him any *way*, Dillon. He kissed me."

He smiled and looked at me beneath his brows. "Come on, Kate. That was a kiss. A real kiss. It doesn't matter who kissed whom. That doesn't have anything to do with it. I only meant that I realized two things in that moment. One—I'm not the man for you. You need someone that can bring about that much abandon in you. Two—maybe that's something I want for myself. Maybe I want someone who wants me as much as you seemed to want his kiss."

His insight hit a little too close to home for me, but I didn't have the energy to analyze precisely why. Instead, I just leaned in to wrap my arm around him in a hug.

"You deserve that, Dillon. I hope you find it very soon."

He kissed the top of my head before stepping away. "Me too, Kate. Take care of yourself, okay?"

I walked him to his car, and as I watched him pull away from Cagair Castle, I felt free of a burden I hadn't known I'd been carrying.

Now, I just needed to deal with my mother.

I made sure to knock on the door this time. I was quite certain I would never open another closed door again without knocking. When my mother opened the door, she was already dressed, with her hair perfectly curled and her bangs pinned back so she could apply her makeup. She smiled guiltily and laughed.

"I'm sure that was quite a shock for you. I really am sorry. That's not at all how either of us wanted you to find out."

"I cannot freaking believe you. I'm not sure I've ever been so angry at you in my whole life."

Her expression immediately changed from one of sorry-not-sorry to confusion. She crossed her arms defensively.

"Look, Kate. I can understand you being a little taken aback, but you have no right to be angry about this. David and I are both grown. It's our business if we decide to spend time with one another."

I shook my head at the irony. "You think I'm angry about David?"

She nodded and I sighed in exasperation. "You really don't have any idea how hypocritical you are, do you, Mom? Of course, I'm not angry about David. I love David. Do I wish I hadn't walked in on the two of you naked? Definitely. But I think you're lucky to have him. David's great. What I'm angry about is why you can so easily see the need for you to have some privacy when it comes to your love life, but you don't see any need to give your daughters the same courtesy."

She let out a loud breath and uncrossed her arms as she nodded knowingly. "You mean Dillon."

"Of course, I mean Dillon. He showed up here this morning, thanks to you."

"Darling..."

I cut her off by screaming. I hated it when she called me darling.

"No! Don't call me darling. This is not okay. Not at all. Do you know what upsets me the most? I don't blame you for liking Dillon. But this wasn't about you and your opinion of him. You don't trust my judgment. You don't trust me to make my own decisions."

She walked past me to sit on the edge of the bed. "I haven't always felt that way, Kate. I used to trust you completely."

I clenched my teeth together in preparation for what I knew was coming. She'd never said the words out loud before, but I'd felt them in so many of her actions. "Oh yeah? And what happened to make you lose that trust?"

"Sweetheart, it's not your fault. But you know as well as I do that you haven't been yourself since the fire. I don't know how you can be sure of any decision that you make until you get back to being yourself."

There it was. The exact thing I always suspected she believed. That the person I was before would someday come back—and that she liked that version of me a whole lot more.

I couldn't even bring myself to be angry with her. It just made me feel sad and wholly inadequate. I could never give her what she wanted.

"Mom, I am myself. My new self. That old me that you used to know—I'm not hiding her anywhere. She just simply doesn't exist anymore. I've changed, and frankly, I like who I am now. I know I still have things I need to work on, but doesn't everyone? Do you really think you'd be able to go through what I did and come out on the other side exactly the same as you are now?"

When she said nothing, I continued. "I like the person I am today. I just wish you did, too."

I turned away and walked toward the door.

"Kate...where are you going?"

"Away from you. I need time alone. I'm going to speak to Maddock and see if we can leave tomorrow instead of today. I'm too angry with you right now to ride next to you all day."

She tried to say something as I walked away, but I was in no mood to stop and listen.

CHAPTER 16

I went back to my room after leaving my mom and took some time to shower and clean myself up—I was still in my pajamas, after all—before knocking on the door that led to Maddock's room from inside our connected bathroom.

When he answered, he was still in his robe. Half of his face was red as if he'd been laying on it, and his hair was smooshed to one side. Clearly, he'd been sleeping. He looked so stinking adorable that I couldn't help but smile, despite my guilt over waking him.

"I'm sorry. Were you sleeping?"

He smiled and nodded. "I was, but I suppose 'tis time we leave, aye?"

"About that...do you think it would be okay if we waited until tomorrow? I think everyone could use one more day of rest before heading out on such a long journey."

His already friendly face lit up completely. "Ach, lass, I could kiss ye again. I doona think I've ever heard a more pleasing suggestion."

"Good." I stood there awkwardly for a moment, unsure of how to thank him for what he'd done before.

"Lass?"

I looked up from staring down at my feet as he spoke. "Yes?"

"How are ye? I saw him leave."

I exhaled again. Every time I thought of Dillon now, I felt a sense of ease. The usual tightness that spread over my chest at any thought of him was gone, and much of that was due to Maddock.

"I'm good. It all worked out okay in the end."

"I'm sorry if I interfered more than I should have."

I shrugged. "Please don't be sorry. While shocking, it was actually the perfect thing to do. It opened up a conversation between the two of us—one that allowed me to forgive him for a hurt."

His brows furrowed in concern. "What did he do to hurt ye?"

I dismissed it with my hand. "It should've been nothing. I don't know why I let it upset me so much. He didn't mean it anyway, but he just mentioned that if I gave him up, I would have trouble finding someone to want me now that I'm..." I hesitated and lifted my amputated arm, "damaged."

Maddock's nostrils flared as the muscles in his jaw bulged. "The man is a foolish bastard. I'm afraid ye shall see just how untrue the arse's words were when we reach the Isle. Every man there will want ye."

I flushed at that, and in my nervousness decided to ignore the latter half of Maddock's statement. "He's not a bastard. He was just hurt and angry at me for leaving him."

Maddock rolled his eyes. "Whatever ye say, lass. I still doona care for him, and I'm pleased he's gone from yer life."

"I am too. And I'm even more glad that I can go through the

rest of my life knowing that we didn't end things by hating each other. Thank you again for what you did."

He smiled that same ornery grin that he'd had just before kissing me. "'Tis I that should be thanking ye. I've not been kissed like that in a verra, verra long time."

I reached for the door in my urgency to step away from him. "I didn't kiss you. You kissed me. Now, get some more rest. Tomorrow will come quickly and neither one of us got any sleep last night."

He laughed as I closed the door between us, and I thought I heard him say once again, "Whatever ye say, lass. Whatever ye say."

Three Days Later—1651

Freezing, soaked to the bone, and with a cough that was beginning to worry me more than I wanted to admit, I trudged my way through the mud back over to my horse after an absolutely miserable stop in the middle of some trees so we could all take a quick pee.

"I know, baby. It's not fun for me, either. We're all moving as quickly as we can."

Mr. Crinkles whined miserably from inside the pocket of my coat that Gillian had sewn for me before we left. Anticipating the weather, she knew he would need a place to keep dry. While I was certain he was grateful for the warmth, he was a cat accustomed to having lots of space to roam around. For days, he'd been cramped up against me.

I knew such a long journey on horseback would be difficult, but each day was more miserable than I could have possibly imagined. Rain poured down on us nonstop. While Maddock and Paton made certain to find us decent lodging each night, the mornings and our journey through the rain always came much too soon.

I ached all over, and each breath seemed much more difficult than it should've been.

I stopped as I reached my horse and waited for Maddock's dutiful assistance. While I could manage riding the horse with one arm fine, I couldn't pull myself up onto the horse with just my left hand. With the way I felt now, I didn't think I would've been able to do it even with two.

"Ye doona look well, lass. 'Tis not too far to the next village. We shall stop early today. I can see that ye need rest."

Maddock stood right behind me, but his voice sounded far away. I leaned back into him as his hands gripped my waist to lift me. As I did so, my cheek brushed against his.

"Ye are burnin' up. Are ye sure ye are…"

That's all I remember hearing before I passed out in his arms.

CHAPTER 17

*K*ate trembled as she slept, and each breath she drew was strained. With her mother sitting on the edge of the bed and her cat curled up at her feet, Maddock paced the small room where they all would stay the night.

Paton caught his eye and motioned for him to join him in the hallway.

Quietly, he slipped away from the group so as not to draw attention.

"We canna heal her, Maddock."

"Aye, I know." He sighed and leaned against the wall. Healing magic would place too much strain on their powers. With The Eight still missing a member and them being so far from the Isle, it could put them in great danger.

Paton continued to ramble on as if he'd not just agreed with him. "Even on the Isle, even with the other men, healing magic is the most difficult. This far from home with only the two of us, such a strain could break our bond to the others. It could set Machara free."

"Aye, I know. Hush yer mouth. I canna think with yer yammering." He didn't need Paton to explain to him what he already knew.

At the rate they were moving now, they were still four days from the Isle. If the weather grew worse or if Kate's sickness remained, it would take them even longer. She might be dead by then.

Unencumbered by new riders and able to ride through the night without sleep, he and Paton had been able to make the entire journey in just three days.

"We canna let Laurel's sister die while in our care."

"Paton." He shoved his friend into the opposite wall and held both his hands on his shoulders. "I've no intention of letting the lass die. We will have to split up so that one of us can get Kate to the Isle more quickly. Then the rest of the men can heal her."

"I'll take her."

Maddock laughed and dropped his hands from Paton's shoulders. There was no way he was letting Kate out of his sight. "I'll be the one taking her. I ride faster than ye do. Besides, the lass is more comfortable in my presence than in yers."

"Ha! How could ye possibly know that? We've both known her exactly the same amount of time. Myla hates me, Maddock."

Maddock smiled for the first time all day. It was true. Kate's mother did seem to despise Paton for some reason none of them could quite understand.

"Trust me, I just know. Besides, Myla's distaste for ye is even more reason that I should be the one to see Kate to the castle. Myla wouldna want her daughter in yer care."

Paton frowned and gave him one begrudging nod. "Aye, fine. When will ye leave with her?"

He could spare a little magic to keep her warm and to help

her rest, but the ride would be taxing on her, regardless of the little comfort he could provide. If she could sleep now, she needed to.

"Morning. For now, I shall inquire with the innkeeper if there is a healer in the village. Mayhap I can find something medicinal to help her with the illness." He stepped away and then paused before Paton walked back inside the room. "Say nothing of this to her mother just yet. It will only make her worry about the severity of Kate's illness. I will tell her just before we leave."

Watching Paton slip back inside with the others, Maddock made his way downstairs where the old man who'd rented them the room sat rocking by the fire.

"Pardon me, sir. I am verra sorry to disturb ye so late, but the lass I carried in has grown worse. Is there a healer close by? I'm afraid 'tis quite urgent that I find some help."

The old man stood and walked over to open the front door, waiting until Maddock stood next to him to point out into the wet, cold night. "Aye, I do. Fourth home to the right. The one with the candle still burning in the window. The lad's name is Brachan. His mother grows the flowers and herbs he uses, and he mixes them on his own. We've not had a villager die here from anything other than old age in three years. If he canna see the lassie well, then I doona believe anyone will be able to."

<hr />

A woman far younger than he expected opened the door after his first knock.

"Doona tell me 'tis Murdock again? I thought we had him well days..." She paused as she stepped forward to look at him more closely, then she smiled and dipped her head in embarrassment. "Ach, ye are not who I thought ye were. My apologies. I've not seen ye around here before. Ye must be passing through, aye? What can we do for ye?"

Maddock stepped into the small cottage as the woman ushered him inside.

"'Tis not for me. I'm traveling with a small group, and one of the women has fallen ill. She has a terrible cough and fever. She drifts in and out of consciousness."

"Well, we canna have that, can we?"

The woman turned away from him to address the man sitting at a table in the far corner of the room with his back toward them. "Brachan, grab yer bag and come and greet this man so ye may follow him to wherever his lady friend lies ill."

"She is not..." He stopped, deciding that was unimportant. Besides, he liked the way that sounded.

Maddock watched on as Brachan slowly stood, reached for a small satchel underneath the desk where he worked, and turned toward him.

"Forgive my rudeness, sir. I was in the middle of mixing a tincture. I would've forgotten where I was had I stood to greet ye the moment ye entered. Now, what else can ye tell me of the woman's symptoms?"

Maddock could find no immediate words as he stared at the man in front of him. Brachan bore a striking resemblance to a younger Nicol. The man had the same green eyes, the same spotty stubble, and the same distinct chin.

"The...she...the lass is trembling all over without end, and as I said, she has a fever and a horrible cough. She passed out in my arms earlier in the day. Might I ask ye lad, what is yer surname?"

"Young. My name is Brachan Young, sir."

Maddock would've bet all he owned that the man would've said Murray, just like Nicol.

"Do ye have relations to the clan Murray? Ye look just like someone I know."

Brachan's mother stepped in between them. Her tone was suddenly far less friendly. "Clan Murray? Why would ye ask that? And what of yerself? What might yer name be, and where are ye from?"

Maddock couldn't understand the woman's sudden change of mood, but he said nothing of it.

"My name is Maddock and I live on The Isle of Eight Lairds. I thought mayhap ye might have relations there, for yer son looks just like my friend and master, Nicol."

The woman's hands moved to his arms as she tried to push him back toward the door. He didn't budge. "Get out of my house, sir. While I hope the lass recovers, we willna be giving her aid."

"If I have done anything to offend ye, I am truly sorry, but I am afraid I canna leave without yer son's help. The lass may truly die without it, and I willna allow that to happen."

Brachan moved toward his mother, placing a gentle hand on her back. "I will help them regardless of where they come from, Mother. We canna live in fear forever. I will be back by morning. Doona wait up."

Maddock turned to follow the man as he brushed past his mother and stepped out of the house.

"The lass is at the inn, aye?"

Maddock called after him as Brachan moved in that direction. "Aye, first room at the top of the stairs."

Maddock slowed to watch Brachan as he made his way to the inn. The man even ran like Nicol.

If Brachan's appearance hadn't been enough to convince him, the reaction of the boy's mother would've done the job.

Nicol had a son.

One that wasn't Freya's. One that Maddock suspected Nicol knew nothing about.

CHAPTER 18

"There ye are, lass. Sit up and drink this for me. Every bit. I know it tastes horrid, but 'twill help ye with that cough."

Hands were on me, gently lifting me from where I lay on a thin, worn mattress in the middle of some obscure village in the middle of seventeenth century Scotland. So far, this century wasn't treating me too kindly.

I knew I still had a fever. My vision was slightly blurry as I struggled to open my eyes, and I felt so weak I could barely hold up my head.

The man sitting next to me was new, but his eyes were kind and warm and his tone was so reassuring that I didn't doubt his claims that the medicine would help. Shakily, I opened my mouth to accept the wooden cup he brought to my lips. The stench of the thick liquid nearly made me gag, but as I was already warned, I inhaled through my nose and swallowed every drop of the man's potion.

"Thank...thank you."

"No need, lass. 'Twill make ye sleepy. Doona fight it. I'll be here when ye wake up. We will see how ye are feeling then."

Whatever was in the concoction worked quickly, as my eyes were already drifting closed.

---

*B*y the time I woke, it was morning. When I opened my eyes, I was no longer worried I would die. My fever had broken, and I was able to push myself up. Mr. Crinkles crawled up my legs to collapse in my lap and purr. He'd been worried. And so had my mother, if the tears running down her face were any indication. But instead of kissing me, she walked right over to the medicine man, threw her arms around him, and kissed his cheeks up and down.

"Thank you, thank you, thank you. Is she well? Will she live? I mean, I can see that she's much better, but is she...is she out of the woods yet?"

My mom continued to ramble as the saintlike-in-his-patience man slowly peeled my mother off him and stepped closer to me.

"Ye needn't thank me. I willna be able to tell ye anything until I've examined her more closely. Could ye all step outside a moment?"

Mom nodded and ushered everyone outside. I wasn't sure I'd ever seen her move so quickly.

Once we were alone, the man walked over to the bed and gently laid one hand on my calf. "Can ye sit all the way up for me, lass? I need to see ye in better light."

It took some effort, but I managed to prop myself up, slide my legs out, and sit on the bed's edge mimicking him.

"What's the verdict? I'll live, right? I really do feel much better."

He smiled, and it made his green eyes pop amongst his mass of already-graying hair. He looked so familiar and not in the sense that I'd seen someone that looked like him before. I had the overwhelming sense that I'd seen *him* before.

"Ye would've lived without my assistance, though I do believe ye shall heal more quickly now. Might I..." He hesitated and gently lifted his palms very close to my face.

I nodded. "Do whatever you need to. I've had my fair share of experience with doctors."

"Doctors?"

I quickly corrected myself. "Healers."

"Ah. Is that what Old Man Wilson told ye I was?" He moved his hands to either side of my face, gently cupping it as he lifted my chin and examined me. "They're all so protective of me."

I looked down at him as he lifted my chin. "Aren't you?"

Rolling his hands forward, he moved my chin down so that I stared straight at him. He looked into my eyes for a minute as if he were looking for something within my pupils.

"Aye, I can be when 'tis necessary for me to be."

I found the strange man intriguing. Other than his graying hair—although, even that suited him—he appeared quite young, but he didn't come across as young in the way he spoke or carried himself. He reminded me of Laurel in that sense—a bit of an old soul in a young body.

"And what are you when it isn't necessary for you to be a healer?"

He didn't answer me. Instead, he dropped his hands from my face and nodded toward the elbow on my left arm. "How often does that burn hurt ye?"

I frowned suspiciously at him. I'd just been thinking to myself that it was aching again, but my arm was covered by my dress, and I didn't think I'd held it funny or gestured to it in any way. How did he even know it was hurting me? And how on Earth did he know that it was one of the very few spots on my body where I'd actually been burned in the fire?

"Excuse me?"

"The burn, lass. It hurts ye, aye? I can help ye with that. Turn around and allow me to loosen yer gown so ye may pull yer arm through the top."

I didn't move. I just stared at him with shocked eyes.

"Wha...how did you?"

He quickly dismissed me as he reached behind and began to undo my laces.

"Doona worry. I doona mean to be forward. I just wish to examine the burn."

It hadn't even occurred to me that he had. I had a hoard of overbearing, worried companions right outside the door. Besides, he just didn't seem the type.

"I'm not worried about that. How did you know there was a burn there?"

He gave me a stare that made it very clear he had no intention of answering my question as my gown loosened at the top and I pulled my arm through.

Once he held the arm, he moved his fingers to the wide burn that spread across the back of my arm. Gathering the seared flesh he pinched it so hard I nearly cried.

"Ow." I jerked away from him. "What are you doing? That hurts."

He gave one curt nod. "Aye, I know. Would ye rather a brief moment of pain now or longer moments of pain for the rest of yer life?"

I frowned and hesitantly offered him my arm. "I don't see how pinching it is going to do anything."

He grabbed onto the damaged skin once again. Although he

didn't let go, his eyes did soften when he saw that I was stifling a groan.

Eventually, the pain turned to warmth, and by the time he released my arm, it no longer ached at all.

I wanted to rub the spot, but since my lack of another hand prevented me from doing that, I simply twisted the arm around. I could feel nothing. It felt entirely normal.

"What did you do?"

He shook his head in another non-answer.

"I must go. I've already stayed longer than I said I would. Ye will live, lass. I see no more sickness inside ye, but ye shall be weak for a few days still. Ye shouldna spend much time out of doors for the next fortnight, or ye could risk falling ill again. 'Twas a pleasure to meet ye."

I twisted my head in confusion as he neared the door.

"Did we actually meet? I don't remember telling you my name."

Just as his hand reached for the door, he twisted back and gave me a shy smile.

"Ye dinna, Kate. Good day to ye."

He left without another word.

CHAPTER 19

*M*yla wasn't pleased with their plan, but Maddock could tell by the look of resignation in her eyes that she agreed it was the only thing to do under the circumstances. Even though Kate was much improved, four more days of riding through rain and mud in freezing temperatures would do nothing to help with her recovery.

"Fine. I know that David and I can't keep up with the speed that Kate needs us to be moving. But Maddock, I swear to you, if she dies on the way to the castle while under your care, I will kill you myself."

He believed her. The woman had a fire in her eyes that sent a chill down his spine.

"I swear to ye that I will see her safely to the Isle. By the time the rest of ye arrive, she shall be rested and fully recovered. Ye have my word."

"I will keep you to it. When will you leave?"

He'd readied his horse and gathered food from the village while Brachan had examined Kate this morning.

"As soon as ye've said goodbye to her, I shall collect her and carry her downstairs."

While Myla and David spoke with Kate, Maddock went to see to one last thing he hoped would make the hard ride a little easier. Earlier that morning while gathering bread and dried fish for their trip, he'd noticed a small wooden box that was just the perfect size for Kate's beloved cat, out in front of the inn. The old man—just like he'd been the night before—was sitting by the fire.

"Thank ye for telling me of the healer. The lass is much improved."

The man turned toward him with a smile. "I told ye. All in this village stay fine and well because of that lad and his mother. Will ye be leaving today?"

"Aye, sir. Might I ask ye...do ye have any attachment to the wee wooden box just outside?"

The innkeeper's thick, wiry brows pulled together. "I doona even know which box ye speak of. If ye need it, 'tis yers."

Stepping outside, Maddock gathered the box and hurried to the small stable where they'd boarded their horses. There was a brief break in the rain, and he hoped to leave with Kate before it began to pour once more.

"Stella, lass." He stroked his beloved horse gently. "Ye must ride hard and fast for us this day and part of the next. And please doona buck off this wee box I mean to strap to ye. 'Twouldn't do for us to allow harm to come to Kate's cat." He leaned in to nuzzle into her neck. "If ye behave, I shall give ye a bushel of apples when we arrive home."

The horse neighed. Assuming he had permission, he took straps of leather from his satchel and stabilized the box just behind Stella's saddle. Once it was secure, he took some hay from around Stella's feet and placed it in the box to form a bed.

Maddock laughed as Stella turned her head as if she meant to look back and see what he'd done to her. "Just one last touch, lass, and I shall have to go get the wee beastie ye shall carry along with us."

Taking his dagger, he cut off a wide piece of his kilt. It no longer looked as nice, but as long as there was still fabric to cover him, he didn't mind.

Taking the plaid fabric, he folded it twice and lay it on top of the hay to form a bed for the one-eyed feline.

"Ye sit tight, Stella. I'll just be a moment."

Grabbing one of the dried fish and a small wooden bowl from his belongings, he made his way back to the inn where the old man graciously poured a wee dram of milk into the bowl for him to take upstairs to Kate's room. She was awake and looked much more like herself when he entered. She immediately tried to dissuade him from his plan.

"I really do think I'd be okay if we stayed with the rest of the group."

Ignoring her, he set the bowl down on the floor, lay the dried fish next to it, and grabbed Mr. Crinkles off the bed.

The cat meowed. As he placed the creature down by the food, it quickly began to lap it up.

Kate's bare feet appeared in his line of sight as he crouched down next to the cat.

"Oh, Maddock. Thank you so much. I've been slipping him bits of food I packed for him from my own time, but I know he's grateful. This trip has been misery for him."

He looked up at her as he rose from his place on the floor and smiled.

"It has been misery on us all, lass. Most of all ye. Which is precisely why we must separate from the group. I doona believe ye've strength enough to last on the road another four days.

Doona worry. Ye willna have to leave yer wee cat behind. I've made him something that will keep him dry, warm, and will allow him to at least stand and turn around should he need to."

Kate's eyes lit up at his words. The sight of her smiling again after so many hours of being frightened for her health pleased him to no end.

"What is it?"

"Ye shall see as soon as ye've finished dressing and are ready to go."

"I am dressed."

He pointed to the bare feet sticking out from underneath her dress. "I'll not be letting ye ride in this weather with yer feet uncovered."

Kate nodded and moved back to the edge of the bed. "Would you mind sending my mother back in? Normally, I could manage just fine, but I'm still very shaky. I'm afraid if I bend over and attempt to slip those boots on, I'll faint again."

He shook his head and reached for the pair of delicate boots sitting by the door.

"All ye need is to slip them on, aye? I can help ye with that." He hesitated. "If ye doona mind, that is."

She shook her head and lifted her leg. "I don't."

He grabbed the thick wool stockings Sydney had given them and bent at Kate's feet. There was something oddly intimate about sliding the fabric over her feet. It made him warm, and suddenly all of his clothes felt tight. He needed to distract himself, lest he start panting right in front of her.

"What did Brachan say to ye? Did he give ye any remedy to take again or tell ye anything to do that might help?"

Kate sighed, and the breathy sound only increased his discomfort as he pulled the sock up to her knee.

"Brachan, is it? Well, I'm glad someone knows his name. He

didn't tell me much of anything. He just looked at my face for a while and then pinched the crap out of my arm. Speaking of which, look at this. It's incredible."

He looked up as she pulled her arm from its sleeve and popped it out the top of her dress. He gasped as the fabric nearly fell free down her front, but she quickly caught it with her arm. God help him, what was the lass doing? Not only did he have his hands near her thigh, but her gown was undone as well.

"What are ye...what are ye doing, Kate?"

"Look at this." She lifted her left arm, and with the stub of her right arm gently touched her left elbow to direct his attention there. He looked up at the pale flesh and shrugged in confusion.

"What am I meant to see, lass?"

"I had a burn there. One of only three I received from the fire. Touch it. It's smooth now, right? It doesn't just look that way? The burn is gone, isn't it?"

Taking a breath to steady himself, he reached toward the tender side of her arm and brushed his fingers against the flawless skin. He knew of no herbs or tinctures capable of healing wounds so well.

"'Twas it truly burned, lass? For there is no sign of it now."

Her tone was entirely sincere. "Yes, I swear that it was. How could he do that? What sort of herb or whatever you guys use in this time could do that?"

Maddock shook his head. There was only one thing that could provide such results so quickly. The mystery surrounding Nicol's son seemed to thicken with every passing second.

"No salve did that, lass. He used magic. Quite powerful magic, at that."

CHAPTER 20

*B*rachan braced himself as he stepped back inside their small home in the heart of the village. He knew his mother worried for him, but turning away those in need of his help was no way to protect him.

"Ach, there ye are. If ye hadna walked in that door just now, I meant to go and look for ye myself. What is the matter with ye, lad? Ye put yerself in danger last night. And for what? For the sake of some lass ye doona even know? Ye are a fool."

He was weary from his night of keeping watch over the girl, but he had far too many questions to sleep. The travelers at the inn were a key to his past, to who he truly was. His mother's panicked reaction to Maddock's mention of the Isle had revealed that much to him. It was time for his mother to tell him the rest.

"I was in no danger amongst them. Where is Willy?"

"With his sheep. He left to work them at dawn."

He nodded and reached for his mother's hand as he led her to the two chairs near the fire. "Good, then ye may finally tell me the truth. The man Maddock claimed I resembled—Nicol Murray. He is my father, aye?"

His mother said nothing as she bent her head and began to cry.

———

"*T*here is no way in hell I'm letting you carry me down these stairs."

I planted both feet and gripped at the doorway with my left hand so he couldn't pull me away from it.

"Kate, lass, doona be so prideful. Ye are as weak as a babe and are trembling as ye stand."

"I am not..." I paused as my vision whirled and my knees buckled just a bit. It only lasted a moment, but before I could take a deep breath and regroup, Maddock already had me in his arms.

"I know ye doona take well to being ordered about, but for the next day and a half, ye will have to listen to what I tell ye to do. We will ride hard for the Isle, and I will rarely need to stop, so if ye need to halt, ye must say so."

Mom, David, and Paton had already led their horses into the village and were readying to begin their longer ride to the Isle via the main trail. Maddock, Mr. Crinkles, and I would take a more perilous, but faster, route.

Once we were inside the stable, Maddock slowly lowered me to my feet next to the old, gentle horse I'd ridden this far.

"How do ye feel? Are ye steady?"

"I'm fine." I reached out to pat the horse. "What will happen to this guy? We're not taking him with us, are we?"

Maddock shook his head and bent to pick up Mr. Crinkles who'd dutifully followed us all the way out of the inn and into the stables. "No, I've paid a lad from the village to see the horse back to Cagair. Here. Come and see what I did for the wee beastie."

Mr. Crinkles meowed as Maddock lifted him—I was slightly concerned that my cat liked Maddock more than he did me—and placed him in a small wooden box that was turned so that its top faced the front of the horse.

With Maddock riding in front of the opening, Mr. Crinkles would be warm while still having plenty of air and room to stand up and move about just a little. Most importantly, he would be dry.

Mr. Crinkles stood cautiously inside the small box and then walked deeper inside and curled up on what looked like part of Maddock's kilt. He began to purr in appreciation.

It was perfect. Maddock's thoughtfulness blew me away. I walked over to stand in front of him and wrapped my left arm around his neck in a hug. "I think I could kiss you. Thank you so much. It's incredible."

He stiffened just a little as I clung to him. "Ye could what, lass? Last time I said the same to ye, ye grew nervous."

Affectionate by nature, I was prone to hugging strangers and quite often greeted close friends with a kiss. I'd thought nothing of my comment.

Suddenly self-conscious, I hurried to rectify what I'd just walked into. "I didn't get nervous. I just…"

He laughed as he stepped back from our hug. "Ye were just worried if I kissed ye again, ye might fall for me."

I gaped awkwardly before he winked playfully and hurried to brush both hands together before moving to pat his horse. "This here is Stella. She is the finest horse in all of Scotland, and she has already promised me to be kind to both ye and Mr. Crinkles, but we must first decide how ye will ride."

Thankful that he'd changed the conversation, I was more than happy to oblige his leading statement.

"How I'll ride? Do I have options?"

"Oh, aye. Ye most certainly do. The priority must be that ye are as comfortable as ye can be. We canna have ye putting strain on yerself in any way. Do ye wish to face me or the trail?"

It had never occurred to me that facing him was an option. It would be an awkward position to be sure. My legs would have to be situated around his lap, as if I were sitting on him and... ahem...straddling him, but I could see why he offered. If I rode with my back toward him, the frigid wind would whip my face the entire way, which would do nothing to prevent me from getting sick again. If I rode facing him, I could burrow my head in his chest, which would keep me much warmer. It would also be much easier to sleep that way.

"Umm...facing you, if you don't mind?"

"'Tis the only sensible thing for ye to do, lass. Will ye allow me to strap ye to me?"

I laughed because I thought he was joking, but fell silent when he pulled out a long belt-like piece of leather. "Oh, you're serious? Why do you need to do that?"

"So ye can rest. Otherwise, ye will have to hold on the whole way. 'Twill also make it easier for me to concentrate on the ride, lass. I willna worry about ye sliding off of Stella. She'll be kind to ye, but if she is in the midst of a run, she willna stop for ye."

I nodded curtly as he mounted the horse with ease and extended both hands down to me.

"Stand on the tips of yer toes, lass, so I can reach underneath yer arms."

It wasn't the easiest position from which to lift me, but he managed surprisingly well. Feeling rather scandalous, I swung my legs open and lay them around his own as I snuggled in close and bent to tuck my head into his chest as he wrapped the long belt around us.

"People are going to think we are crazy if they see us like this. With Mr. Crinkles on the back and us strapped together, we look like we belong in the circus."

He laughed, and the warmth of his breath tickled the top of my head.

"They willna see us long enough to think anything. Stella moves much too quickly when bribed with a bushel of apples. We will be little more than a blur on the horizon."

CHAPTER 21

The wind, the rain, and the utter misery of the cold were not enough to keep him distracted from the feelings caused by having Kate pressed so closely to him. Warm and soft, the nearness of her flooded his mind with thoughts that made him ache with need. Visions of what she would look like beneath him, pressed even closer together than they were now, filled his mind each time she shifted against him.

Her hair smelled like flowers, and the soft, even rhythm of her breathing was warm against his chest.

What would she do if he tugged ever so gently on that hair as he tilted her head back so he could press his lips to hers like he'd done only a few days before? Would her breathing grow uneven with need like his was now?

Days ago, he wouldn't have doubted it. She'd enjoyed their shared kiss as much as he had, but now she was colder, more distant, and he couldn't figure out why.

Had she grown less fond of him after spending more time in his presence? Or was it perhaps the cruelness of Dillon's words to her that still hindered her confidence?

Whatever it was, he couldn't wait until they reached the Isle. Once there, he would make it his mission to break through whatever kept her so guarded.

It was nightfall now, and they'd made faster time than he'd expected. They would make it to the Isle by sunrise. For the first time in hours, there was a break in the rain, and he slowed Stella's pace so they could enjoy the brief respite from the downpour.

"Are ye awake, lass? Do ye need to walk around a bit? If so, 'twould be best to do so now before the rain starts again."

"No. Keep going." Her answer came out muffled against his chest. She'd barely moved since they'd started their ride.

"Are ye certain?"

"Yes. I'm just ready to get there. Only stop if the horse needs to."

In an effort to keep her spirits up, Maddock playfully chided her. "The least ye can do is call her Stella, lass. Ye wouldna like it if I referred to yer beloved Mr. Crinkles as *the cat,* aye?"

With her head tucked tightly against his chest, she laughed. "You're right. Ask Stella if she needs to stop for a bit. Otherwise, let's just get this over with."

"If Stella needed to rest, she would. She is a loyal and dependable steed, but she has a mind of her own."

He gathered the reins into one hand so he could reach up to brush her hair back with the other. He'd only meant to check for a fever by gently kissing her forehead, but as his fingers brushed against her cheek, he felt Kate's breath come more quickly against his chest and he smiled. She still wanted him. Her pulse gave it away. Mayhap she just needed to know that he wanted her, as well, to feel safe enough to open up to him as she had that first night once again.

"I mean to kiss ye just here, lass." He tapped his thumb

gently to the center of her forehead. "To make certain ye've still no fever."

She nodded and lifted her head from his chest just a bit.

He kissed her, but lingered close to her brow as he pulled his lips away.

"No fever. Lass?"

She smiled and every muscle in his stomach coiled. "Mmm?"

"Ye feel bonny, lass. The weather is pure misery, and Stella's bony back is making my arse ache, but even still, I enjoy the feel of having ye close to me. I'm sorry if the uneven beat of my heart has kept ye awake. Each time I look down at ye, it betrays me by speeding up."

He expected her to respond in some way—to at least smile and shyly lean into him again—but instead she said the last thing he'd ever expected.

"When we get to the Isle, I want you to take me to meet Machara."

She might as well have slapped him in the face. His moment of vulnerability had been received with a closed heart.

The sun was just peeking over the horizon. The shoreline and the boat that would take them to the Isle were barely visible in the distance. At least he wouldn't have to dwell over her rejection of him too much longer.

"While I canna imagine why ye wish to meet her, and while I can think of nothing I wish less than for ye to stand in front of that evil creature, I know such a meeting is inevitable. Ye willna have to wait long." He pointed to the shoreline. "We are almost there."

The Isle of Eight Lairds

They must've heard us coming, or perhaps one of the other members of The Eight had some sort of spidey-sense that alerted them to our arrival, for a group of smiling faces awaited us as we rode up to the castle's stables.

Laurel stood in front, and a man I could only assume was Raudrich had one arm draped over her shoulder as he held her close against him. She was smiling, but as she noticed that no other horses were pulling up behind us, her smile shifted into an expression of concern.

"Did Mom and David not come?"

Maddock dismounted and reached inside Mr. Crinkles' makeshift den and quickly set him on the ground so he could stretch and move his little legs. He answered Laurel as he turned back toward Stella and lifted his arms to help me down.

"Kate fell ill on the journey. She is better now, thanks to a gifted healer we met along the way, but I still thought it best to ride ahead with her to reduce her exposure to the elements. The others are still a day or two behind."

Laurel rushed over to me and threw her arms around my neck. "How are you feeling?"

"Honestly, perfect. Just tired from riding."

As Laurel squeezed me, Marcus slowly approached. I gently pushed my sister away so I could move into his open arms.

"Marcus." I leaned into him and smiled. "You look different —good different, though. How are you taking everything?"

He shrugged. "I'm okay. I'm adjusting to it a little more every day. As resistant as I was to it, there are some cool perks to having powers. You know, you look different, too."

Maddock laughed as I turned to see Laurel bend to pick up Mr. Crinkles and smother him in kisses.

"The lass let loose some baggage 'twas weighing her down."

Laurel turned wide eyes on me. "Dillon?"

I nodded and Laurel simply shrugged. She wasn't nearly as pushy as our mother.

"If you're happy to be rid of him, I'm happy for you."

Bending, Laurel released Mr. Crinkles, who was wagging his tail as he prepared to swat her. "Let's get you into a bedroom, okay? I'm eager to talk with you, and you need some rest anyway. You can meet everyone else later."

"What? No." I looked over at the group of men standing to our right, watching us converse. They were all right here, and it would be silly for me to walk right past them just so I could nap. "I want to meet them now."

A man both shorter and older than the rest, with wavy gray hair that reached his shoulders and eyes that seemed remarkably familiar, stepped forward to greet me. "We are eager to meet ye, as well, Kate. I'm Nicol." Bending toward me, he kissed my cheek, gave me a small smile, and stepped out of the way so the others could come forward.

The moment he stepped back, I gasped. I knew where I'd seen his eyes before—in Brachan. They looked remarkably similar. Too similar for it to be a coincidence. They were undoubtedly related, and I couldn't help but wonder how. Was Nicol an uncle or perhaps a brother? Did Nicol have magic too? Was there any way....I cut the thought off—It wasn't possible for Brachan to be Nicol's son. Was it?

I didn't have long to ponder the multitude of questions that popped into my mind. As soon as Nicol stepped away, the others came forward.

One by one, each of the men greeted me in his own way. They were all so different, but equally kind. I looked forward to getting to know each of them.

By the time Laurel began to usher me inside, Maddock was standing far away from the group with Nicol. Both of their faces were serious, their tones hushed.

I could think of nothing that had happened on our journey that would require such secrecy, but the sight of them piqued my curiosity and started my wheels turning.

"*I* doona care how urgent ye believe this is, doona ye dare say a word of it now."

Maddock glared at Nicol in disbelief. "What do ye mean doona speak of it? 'Tis something ye must know, Nicol."

Nicol remained unmoved. "We have all been through much these past weeks, Maddock. We lost one of our own, Laurel was given a terrible fright, Raudrich was run right through by the woman he loved, Machara nearly broke free, and now after days of turmoil and worry, Raudrich and Laurel are to be wed. Whatever 'tis ye need to say can wait."

Maddock thought of the boy who looked so much like their Master. He had no doubt Brachan was Nicol's son, but what did the power the boy possessed mean? Was he simply another born with power like the rest of The Eight? Many of their parents—like Nicol—lacked magical abilities of their own. Mayhap in a time before Freya, Nicol found company with another lass, and by coincidence their child possessed powers.

But what if the child was something else? What if Machara had deceived them all? What if one of her children with Nicol still lived? If so, there was no way for them to know what sort of threat the boy might pose to them.

"Nicol, I truly doona think it wise to wait for us to address—"

Nicol interrupted him. "Enough. I'll not listen to ye a moment more. I've told ye precisely what ye will do. Ye will keep whatever news ye may have to yerself until Laurel and Raudrich are wed and away from here. We shall have a few days of peace. That is the end of it. Do ye understand me?"

He didn't like it. Not one bit. But perhaps it wasn't as urgent a matter as he thought.

After all, the boy was past twenty. He'd lived many years and posed no threat.

What would cause things to change now?

An Unnamed Village on the Scottish Mainland

*I*t was almost as if his mother's confession had awakened a beast inside him. He could hear the voice dripping with malice as he slept. It called his name over and over and over.

"Brachan...Brachan...Brachan..."

And finally, as he woke covered in sweat and shaking from fear,

"'Tis time, lad. Come home to me."

.

CHAPTER 23

*L*aurel gave me no time to enjoy or explore the castle's surroundings as she held me by my hand and pulled me inside, Mr. Crinkles hot on our heels.

She walked me up the large staircase just inside the entryway and then turned toward the hallway on the left, not stopping until we got to a large door. She pushed it open and yanked me inside. Mr. Crinkles barely managed to make it inside before Laurel slammed the door.

"Whose room is this?"

"This is Maddock's room."

Of course it was.

"Laurel, I really don't want to intrude on his space. Where will he sleep?"

She waved a hand dismissively and turned to jump onto the large bed at the back of the room. "He won't mind at all. He can stay in Paton's room until he gets back with Mom and David. After that, we will figure out something else."

Laurel looked as happy as I'd ever seen her as she sat cross-legged on the bed. She motioned for me to join her.

"I think this time suits you, sis."

She beamed and reached for my hand. "I think it's going to suit you, too. What do you think of Maddock?"

I knew she only asked because it was obvious that I'd spent more time with him than anyone else I'd met so far, but the question made me self-conscious.

"What do you mean?"

Laurel shrugged. "Nothing. I just wondered if you two were getting along. I think he's great."

I nodded and tried not to act squirmy. I didn't succeed. "I agree. He's...he's great."

Laurel gave me a quick knowing glance, and then reached for Mr. Crinkles as he jumped onto the bed. "Okay, I can see something's going on there, but I'm not going to push. Just so you know though—I've gotten to know Maddock very well. I promise you, he's one of the good ones."

I already knew that. "I know."

She raised her brows and nodded. "You want to change the subject?"

"Yes, please."

She laughed. "All right. How did Mom and David take the news about the time travel, the magic, my engagement?"

I smiled thinking back on their casual, carefree reactions thanks to Morna's magic elixir.

"About that...I don't want you to get angry, but I had a little help from Morna. She came by the apartment before you called me for the first time after traveling back here."

"What?"

If Laurel was that surprised by that, I couldn't imagine how shocked she'd be when I told her about our mother and David.

Before I could continue, Laurel interjected once again.

"Please tell me you're joking. She was there, and she wouldn't do anything to help me?"

"She couldn't." I went on to explain to her all that Morna had told me—the reasons why Morna couldn't provide more help or intervene any more than she did. As I told my story, she visibly relaxed.

"Well, at least her lack of assistance wasn't because she doesn't care. So, how did she help you tell Mom and David about everything?"

"She sent a potion that I put in their coffee before we got on the plane. So, remarkably, they seem pretty cool with everything. Although...I have one other doozy of a bomb to drop on you."

"Oh yeah?" Laurel looked intrigued.

"Mom and David...they're um...they're dating or something?"

Her eyes just about doubled in size. "Shut up."

"I'm totally serious, Laurel."

"What do you mean *or something?*"

"Well, I haven't really had a chance to visit with either one of them about it. I only found out because I walked in on the two of them naked. Then Mom and I had a big blow up that caused me to not speak to her for the better part of two days. By the time I'd cooled down enough to get curious, I was too sick to think coherently."

Laurel shook her head and grinned. "Marcus is gonna freak."

I agreed. Not that Marcus would mind it any more than we did, but there was no way he had even the slightest clue.

"I'll let you be the one to tell him. Each time I bring it up, flashes of Mom's bare breasts and David's hands splayed over his crotch fill my mind."

Laurel made a gagging expression and shook her head. "Ew. Just ew. Can I ask...what did you two have a fight about?"

"I broke up with Dillon several weeks before we left for

Scotland. Mom convinced him to fly out to Cagair Castle to try and get me back."

Laurel covered her face with her hands. "Oh my gosh, Kate. I'm so sorry."

I shrugged. "It shouldn't have surprised me."

"Maybe not. It's still not okay." She paused and bit down on her lower lip nervously.

I could tell right away there was something else she wanted to say. "What is it, Laurel?"

"I'm surprised you broke up with Dillon."

I was still kind of surprised myself. "Why?"

She hesitated and crawled off the bed so she could stand and look down at me while she spoke. "Look. I don't want you to take this the wrong way. I love you, and I swear, I'm not trying to be like Mom, but sometimes it's hard for us to see things when we're in the middle of them."

I exhaled and waved her on with my hand as I prepped for unwanted feelings. "Just get on with it, Laurel."

"Dillon didn't challenge you. It was easy with him. You've had so much to deal with since the fire, so it's not as if I blame you, but you do like to take the easy route now."

"Easy?" I exploded off the bed, and Laurel stepped quickly away. "I've done nothing but work my ass off since the fire. I've spent every single day trying to learn how to live with this." I pointed to my missing arm.

Laurel looked at me sympathetically, keeping her calm despite my sudden anger. "I know that. When it comes to your health, your mobility, your independence—your determination has been astounding. You know that's not what I meant. I meant that when it comes to dealing with the tough stuff—your emotions—you've become a pro at checking out. Dillon made it easy for you to do that."

I knew she was right. It didn't make it any easier to hear—
even if it was coming from the one person I knew I could be
honest with.

"Laurel." I started to cry as she moved toward me and
wrapped me up in her arms. "I don't know if I can handle it. I'm
so scared that I'm not strong enough."

She gently kissed the top of my head as she stroked my hair.
"Strong enough for what, Kate?"

"To feel anything again. To stop distracting myself with
everyone else's problems. If I feel *anything*, I have to feel
everything. I'm still so angry about what happened. I don't want
to feel that. I'm afraid that anger will eat me up if I let myself
feel it. I don't want to think about how heartbroken I was when
I woke up. I don't want to feel that way again. Right now I have
a wall up, but each day it's crumbling a little more. If it falls and
I can't keep the feelings at bay anymore, I'm not sure I can come
out the other side of that."

She squeezed me even tighter and then pulled away to hold
me at arm's length.

"You are the strongest person I know. You put up that wall to
help you survive, but your life is no longer at risk. What you feel
can't kill you, Kate. Those emotions, when you decide to let
them in, will make you stronger than you ever thought you could
be. And whoever said the whole dam has to break at once?
When you see an opening to try, just try a little. And when you
survive that feeling, the next one will be a little bit easier."

"Just try, huh?"

She smiled and let go of my arms. "Yes, Kate. Just try."

CHAPTER 24

$\mathcal{H}$e tried to leave it, to do as Nicol ordered, but he couldn't get Brachan off his mind. If Nicol had known what Maddock had been trying to tell him, he wouldn't have been so insistent that they wait until after the wedding to address it. Nicol would want to know. He *needed* to know.

As the sun set behind the castle, Maddock knew there was only one place that Nicol was likely to be—in the withered, long-forgotten garden with Freya. Killed and cursed by Machara, the spirit of their Master's wife now roamed the castle gardens at night, and each evening Nicol walked down to spend the evening with her.

Maddock heard voices the moment he reached the garden, but Nicol's wasn't among them. Instead he heard Freya, her melodic tone welcoming and warm, laughing as she spoke to Marcus, Laurel's best friend and the newest member of The Fight

Maddock spoke the moment he could see them, sitting on the edge of a long-since dried up fountain talking like old friends.

"Ye are not the one I expected to find here, Marcus. Where is Nicol?"

Marcus pointed to the walls of glass on the castle's highest corner—the location of Nicol's bedchamber.

"Sleeping. He woke early so he could greet you and Kate, so I told him that if he needed more rest, that I would come down and visit with Freya for awhile."

Freya smiled at him, but shook her head. "Not that I'm not pleased to have ye here, Marcus, but 'tisn't necessary. I truly doona need to have someone with me every moment that I am here." She paused and patted the stone next to her. "Come and join us, Maddock. Tell me all about yer journey to collect our newest resident."

Maddock did as Freya asked and dove into an explanation of much that had occurred over the past few days—the wonders of seeing a small part of the twenty-first century, the hard journey, and Kate's illness—although his mind was elsewhere as he spoke. When he finished, he realized he couldn't recall much of what he'd said.

He looked up to see Freya watching him thoughtfully.

"What is it, lad? What is on yer mind so?"

Marcus gave a short chuckle and knowingly crossed his arms. "I know that look. That's the look of a man perplexed by a woman. It's Kate, right? She's twisted you all up."

Freya smiled and leaned into him, and part of her shoulder simply disappeared as their figures touched. He could feel nothing, but he understood her gesture.

"Ah come, Maddock. Do tell me. I love a good love story. Mayhap I can even give ye some advice."

Maddock shook his head at Freya's reference. "'Tis hardly a love story yet, lass."

She smiled at him. "But ye'd like it to be?"

Maddock glanced nervously at Marcus. Both Kate and Laurel spoke of Marcus with such adoration. He was certain Marcus would be as protective of Kate as he was of Laurel.

Marcus smiled, seemingly understanding his worry. "I love them both, but you can speak freely about them in front of me. I'm probably even more aware of their quirks than you are."

Maddock stood and began to pace in front of them as his confusion surrounding Kate rushed to the surface. "The lass is unlike any I've met before. She is strong and beautiful, although I doona think she recognizes either such quality in herself. She can be so warm and open on one occasion, and the next make a man feel a fool for opening himself up to her. She is filled with wit, and her love for so many things is infectious, but by God, she is infuriating."

Marcus snorted and gave him a knowing grin. "That's a trait all Adams women share."

Freya chimed in. "'Tis a trait all women everywhere share, lads. We are complex creatures. 'Twould do ye both some good to remember that."

Maddock shook his head as he paused and ran both hands through his hair in frustration. "The night I met her, we stayed up all night talking and I never sensed that she was withholding anything from me, but now it seems like the more time I spend with her, the more she pulls away. Each new effort I make is received a little less warmly than the last."

"She's scared, Maddock." Freya made her observation so confidently, as if there were no other possibility.

He watched her for a moment, but before he could respond, Marcus added his agreement. "Freya's right. Before the fire, Kate was the sort of person that dove in head first with everything— her work, relationships, adventures—she feared nothing. The loss of her arm was traumatic for sure, but I'm not even sure that was the worst of it. I think Kate went through life believing it a safe place, one that could only hurt you if you let it. And then, out of nowhere, everything she believed about life was turned upside down. The world was no longer safe. Everything could change in a matter of moments.

"I think perhaps it was too difficult for her to rectify that life was so much more complicated than she always believed it. That it could still be safe and wonderful, but also terrible and tragic, and that one wasn't truly possible without the other. So, she just shut herself off. It was easier to avoid emotion than face her own existential crisis."

Marcus shrugged and continued. "It's not like she's done anything different than what we all do. I think every one of us goes through a time when it's easier to just not feel than to deal with whatever's eating at us, but where Kate got all messed up was that the trauma of that night was so much more than what most of us deal with. She needed to shut some things off just to get herself up in the morning, to deal with the pain of letting herself heal, but she let it go on for far too long, and now it's just a sticky habit that's hard for her to break."

Maddock moved to resume his seat by Freya as he pondered this. It made sense to him. The way she would be receptive to his kiss, but then grow uncomfortable at his mention of it. The way her breath would grow quick against his chest in response to his touch, and then change the subject when he mentioned how she affected him. She wanted to feel, she just no longer held the belief she was strong enough to withstand it.

"How do I help her?"

Freya reached out to lay her ghostly hand up on his knee. "Ye doona give up on her. Ye delight in every instance where she shows ye who she truly is, and ye doona stand for any time that she may put up a false front to protect herself. Let her know that ye want her—the real her—and that ye willna settle for anything else."

He looked over to see Marcus nodding. "Again...she's right. Kate's strong, and it's really the only thing she responds to. She made remarkable progress so quickly in terms of her mobility and adapting to the loss of her arm, and a lot of that was due to the fact that her physical therapist and Laurel never put up with any of her shit. They didn't let her get away with anything. Perhaps, it's time for someone to do that with her feelings, too."

He didn't want to be harsh with her. He wanted to love her, to make her feel cared for, to wrap her up in his arms and kiss every last inch of her.

"She may hate me for it."

Marcus nodded. "She might for a bit, but she'll get over it. Is she worth it?"

He had no doubt that she was.

CHAPTER 25

*M*y intention to ask Laurel about Nicol so I could figure out the possible relation between him and Brachan went out the window after my small breakdown in my sister's arms. We continued to talk with one another for a few more hours, but mainly we spoke of wedding plans and all that had happened to her since she'd been here.

By the time she left me to go to bed, I'd decided to go and look for Maddock to ask him about it. I didn't have to look far. The moment I opened the bedchamber door to step out into the hallway, he was walking by.

"Maddock."

He jumped slightly at the sound of my voice, but smiled as he faced me.

"Kate, lass, I'm pleased ye caught me. There is something I've meant to ask ye all day, but I dinna wish to disturb ye if ye were already asleep."

Intrigued, I waved him inside and closed the door behind him. "I wasn't asleep at all." I motioned around the room.

"Thank you for letting me stay in your room. I really wouldn't mind sleeping somewhere else if you want your space back."

"No, lass. 'Tis no trouble at all. Paton's room will suit me fine, though I'll not be in it long."

"What do ye mean?"

He smiled shyly. "My whole life I've had a problem with walking about while asleep. 'Tis worse when I'm tired, and I canna deny that I am verra tired after our journey."

That surprised me. "How did I not know that?"

"I've not done much sleeping since I met ye, lass. How would ye know?"

That was true. The first night we'd stayed up talking, and I never saw him sleep on the road.

"How are you able to do that? Go without so much sleep, I mean. I'm a monster after just one night of sleep deprivation."

"The magic helps. It can sustain us past what is possible for most."

It was easy to forget that Maddock contained magic. He seemed so normal. I wasn't sure that I'd ever seen him use any.

"Can you not use your magic to keep you from sleepwalking?"

He laughed, but shook his head. "One would think, aye? But alas, since I never know precisely when I might do it, 'tis not worth the effort to cast a spell that might prevent it, especially now that we've only seven men. We canna afford to use magic that isn't necessary."

"I see. What was it that you wanted to ask me?"

He hesitated just long enough for me to see that he was slightly nervous, and it made something inside me coil up with anxiety. "I was only wondering...lass, why did ye ignore me before? Why did ye speak of Machara just as I confessed to ye just how much I enjoyed holding ye close to me?"

My mouth gaped open like a fish as I struggled with how to respond, but before I could, he held up a hand to stop me.

"Doona say anything yet, lass, for I need ye to tell me the truth."

My body began to tremble all over, and I couldn't tell if it was from fear or anticipation—perhaps it was a little of both.

"Why do you need to know that?"

He smiled that familiar mischievous grin and my stomach clenched with need.

"Because, lass, if 'twas a sign of yer disinterest, I shall turn around and walk out this door with nothing but admiration for ye. My friendship will always be yers. But if yer eagerness to change the topic of our conversation this morn was the product of yer fear—if ye do believe ye care for me, I mean to show ye right now just what it could be like between us."

While my desire was to charge him and beg him to take me right there on the floor, my instinct was to shut him down on the spot. But all I could hear was Laurel's voice in my ear, *"Just try, Kate. Just try."*

And so, with shaky breath and trembling hands, I tried to let just a little bit of feeling into my mind and heart. "I...I care, Maddock. I didn't say anything because I knew you could feel my breath shaking against your chest. I thought maybe you were just being polite—trying to make me feel better about myself."

He smiled, and the expression on his face sent chill bumps down my spine. There was nothing friendly in his smile. It was threatening, dangerous, and so sexy. I worried that if he actually made it across the room to touch me, I would unravel before him.

"Lass, never in my life have I been known as polite. Kind? Aye. Decent? I hope. But I doona care for polite. Polite implies that I've a passive nature. If ye expect me to be passive with my feelings for ye, Kate, I'm afraid ye will be sorely disappointed."

He stepped even closer. As I tried to scoot away once more, he reached for my wrist and pulled me against him.

Smiling, he leaned down to kiss the side of my neck. The moment his lips touched my skin, I gasped. As his lips traveled up to my ear and nipped at my lobe, I moaned and leaned back into his palms, which were now splayed out against the lower part of my back.

My moan seemed to ignite something in him, and as he pressed me even tighter against him, his lips moved to mine. His kiss was all consuming. A hot fiery thing that so contradicted the gentlemen he'd been until now. Our lips moved together with an urgency that surpassed that which we'd shared in the kitchen at Cagair. I couldn't get enough of him, couldn't get him close enough to my body. As his hand moved to cup my breast, I cried out in need and longing. "Undress me. Please undress me."

Obligingly, he moved to the laces at the back of my gown, but he didn't wait to untie the gown all the way before he began to pull it lower off my shoulders. The moment my breasts sprang free, he groaned and dropped his mouth to them. Just as his teeth latched around one of my nipples, I realized that my desire was just too much. I could feel some piece of myself unraveling. Hurriedly, I pushed him away. "Wait, Maddock."

He stilled and stood immediately. "What is it, lass?"

"I...I don't want this."

He lifted my dress to cover my breasts and nodded calmly. "I'm sorry, lass. 'Twas too much, too soon. Let me go to the kitchen and find us something to eat. We can just sit together and talk. There is no need for us to do anything more."

"No." I shook my head and in my panic, said the one thing I

didn't mean at all. "I didn't mean this. I meant you. I don't want you."

I saw his teeth grind together, but his voice was calm when he spoke. "Aye, ye do, lass. Ye want me so badly ye are scared to death of it. But I've no need of anyone who is so frightened of everything that they are willing to toy with another's emotions just to protect themselves. Goodnight, Kate."

He turned and walked out.

CHAPTER 26

For the better part of two days, I kept a low profile. I didn't know how to remedy the situation with Maddock, and I was worried that if I was out and about the castle, my sour mood would be visible, and I didn't want anyone to have to worry about me.

It surprised me then, to hear his voice on the other side of the door two days after our last encounter.

"Kate, lass, I thought ye might like to know that yer mother and David have arrived."

I opened the door to him and gauged his expression carefully. He looked as friendly as ever.

"Oh, okay. Thanks for letting me know. Should I go down to meet them?"

He shook his head. "I doona think 'twill be necessary. I'm certain yer mother will be headed this way shortly. She is eager to see that ye are well."

"Oh, okay." I repeated myself, unsure of what to say to him. Eventually, in a burst of bravery, I said, "I thought you would be mad at me."

He blinked as his brows furrowed together. "Lass, why would I be angry with ye?"

I shrugged. "Because I told you I didn't want you."

He cocked one knowing eyebrow at me, and I felt my cheeks flush red in embarrassment.

"But ye do, lass. And even if ye dinna want me, I still wouldna be angry with ye."

"If you're not angry, then what are you?"

He smiled and reached out to gently squeeze my hand. "I'm yer friend, lass."

I mimicked his expression, raising one suspicious brow of my own. "So, you're not going to find another reason to kiss me? You're not going to compliment me or say anything flirty?"

He maintained a stoic expression as he dropped my hand. "No, lass. Three times I opened the door for ye, and three times ye turned me away. Ye are not ready. I canna fault ye for that. But our lives are now intertwined, lass. 'Twould be a shame for either of us to harbor ill will toward the other."

Nothing about what Maddock was saying felt right, but I could feel no dishonesty in his gaze or tone.

Before I could respond to him, he pointed toward the end of the hallway where I leaned out from my doorway to see my mother barreling toward me.

"Kate! Oh my God, I'm glad to see you. How are you feeling?"

I smiled as her arms came around me but I quickly pinched my nose at the stench of her.

"Much better. How was the rest of the journey?"

"We survived it. That's all I care to dwell on. Laurel has some large, redheaded man making me a bath so I can wash off all of this mud and dirt, but he pointed me to where I could find you so I ran up here really quickly to check on you and squeeze your neck."

I nodded and pulled out of her grip. "I'm happy to see you, too. Now go get in that bath. You stink." I winked at her and continued. "I'll catch up with you later. I know you must be exhausted."

"I am, dear." She turned her head and gave Maddock a curt nod. "Maddock."

He copied her gesture. "Myla."

As my mother left us, I noticed a foul stench remained long after she disappeared around the corner, and Maddock's jaw grew tight as he scrunched up his nose.

"What is that?"

"Machara. Are ye ready to meet her?"

Before arriving at the castle, I'd been anxious to meet her. I wanted to see firsthand what I would be dealing with. I wanted to get a read on her to see how I could defeat her, but now, I was more nervous than I expected to be.

"I suppose now is as good a time as any. Maddock?"

"Aye, lass?"

"I'm frightened."

He nodded and took off down the hallway, waving his hand so I would follow him. "Ye should be. If Machara dinna frighten ye, I would be afraid of ye."

*N*icol had just awakened from his morning slumber when Maddock knocked on his bedchamber door. He opened it, smiled warmly, and stepped aside to let us inside.

It was a breathtaking room. With two walls made of solid glass, it had a modern appearance that, while at odds with the rest of the castle's gothic décor, somehow blended nicely. It looked out over the castle grounds and an old, wilted garden that I assumed was where Freya appeared at night. I made a mental note to go and meet her that evening.

"I'm afraid she's discovered that sending her vile smell throughout the castle works. We simply canna ignore it forever, and eventually we go down to see whatever 'tis she feels she must say."

Maddock nodded and came to stand beside me as I looked out one of the glass windows.

"Aye. Mayhap if she meets our new residents, she will realize that they are no threat and will go back to searching for some way to destroy us."

Maddock's comment surprised me. For twenty years, The Eight had held Machara as their prisoner beneath the castle, and they were still not free from her. Laurel had only been here a short period of time, and she'd bested the bitch. Clearly, he knew nothing of what Machara's father had cast into existence so many years ago—the chink in Machara's, for lack of a better word, faerie armor that made it possible to defeat her.

"Why do you think I'm no threat to her?"

Both Maddock and Nicol turned to look at me in surprise. Maddock spoke first. "Ye are mortal, lass. Ye have no magic. Ye have no fae blood that we know of. Machara canna be beaten by one like ye. Besides, dinna ye come here to be with yer sister?"

I leaned into the glass wall behind me as I stared at both of them incredulously. They knew nothing. While I knew Laurel had been too busy with her own showdown with the faerie to sit them all down for a nice long chat, I still found it difficult to believe that she'd said nothing to them about what I'd told her. Although, in truth, she knew less about everything than I did.

Still, their attitude toward Machara stunned me. Even the

way they spoke about her made her sound less like their prisoner and more like some queen that had to be obeyed. It was as if they were resigned to the belief that Machara was, and always would be, part of their lives at the castle, as if they had no intention of ever trying to be free of her. Was this the way all of the members of The Eight were? Had this been their way of life for so long that they were resigned to it?

Had they truly convinced themselves that they were content to spend their whole lives keeping Machara locked away with the reward for their hard work being that they would never be free?

I stared at them for a long moment as I worked through all of this in my mind. I wasn't Machara's caretaker. I wasn't going to be her friend. While they might both be fine with coming to her every time she chose to use her horrid stench as some sort of call bell, I wouldn't placate her in such a way.

My earlier fear was gone. So was any desire I had to see her.

"You go and see Machara if you want to. I'll meet her when *I'm* ready."

I turned away and left them without another word as I went in search of the one member of The Eight that was the most likely to still have some hope.

CHAPTER 27

I found Marcus visiting with his dad in the castle kitchen.

"Kate!" Marcus stood and moved to pull me into one of his award-worthy hugs that always made me feel like there was a little more love in the world than I'd felt like there was before he wrapped his arms around me.

"How are you feeling? Still no fever?"

I smiled as I pulled away from him. "Everyone is much too worried about me. I feel perfect now. No fever at all."

David stood and reached out to touch my arm. "Just so you know, I told him. I think your mother is telling Laurel as we speak. As much fun as it was for the two of us to sneak around, I'm pleased that we can now be open about our love for one another."

I decided not to mention to David that I'd already told Laurel. "Well, good."

David gave my arm a gentle pat as he left Marcus and me alone.

The moment David was gone, I turned to Marcus for his

reaction to the news. I recognized the expression of shock on his face all too well.

"Who would've thought, huh?"

I shook my head and laughed, and we sat down together on a long wooden bench. "Not me. But, I guess it's pretty nice, right? Now that I think about it, I think they're sort of perfect for each other."

"Agreed, but that's not what you came to talk to me about. What's up?"

I'd known Marcus for so long there was no need for me to beat around the bush with him about anything. I got straight to the point.

"Tell me about the druid stuff. Why do they refer to themselves as druids? How did you know you were one? What did you learn when they took you away? Are you happy doing this? Is this what you want for your life?"

He smiled. "Which one of those do you want me to answer first?"

"Just explain this all to me."

He shifted as he settled in to get a little more comfortable before beginning. "Okay. Well, as for the term *druid*, we don't use it in the traditional sense. We're really witches or sorcerers," he paused and scrunched up his nose, "or would it be wizards?" He shrugged, gave me a quick smile and continued. "I'm really not sure. Point being, druids come from an ancient Celtic religion and are often known for their ability to heal or give counsel. They observe the solstices and equinoxes with special ceremonies.

"We do all of these things, too. We each hold an equal stake in the land here, so as lairds of the Isle we often give counsel and help in the management of the land. We heal those who are sick, although most of the time we don't use magic for that. We also observe the changes of the seasons and moon cycles. But…" He held up a finger as he made his point. "We don't practice the true druid religion. Our powers are just inside us, and we're not sure where they come from or why."

I held up my hand to stop him so I could ask a question. "So, even back home in Boston, you had magic inside you and didn't know it."

He nodded. "I guess so. That's the issue Dad has, I think. He can't seem to wrap his mind around it. And if I hadn't been able to feel the magic awaken itself in me once I got here, I'm not sure I would've believed it either. In all honesty, there's so much that we don't know or understand about what we are. All of it is conjecture. Nicol has a theory, though. He believes that more people than you would think have these abilities, but most are never in a situation that calls up the magic inside of them."

I interrupted him once more. "So, it just lies dormant until needed? And for most people—especially, in our time—that's pretty much forever?"

"Exactly."

"What about when they took you away for training? What did they tell you about your role here? Your purpose?"

He waited a moment. "Most days they just focused on helping me hone my powers. They did, of course, explain the duty we have to the Isle, and that our combined magic helps keep everyone that lives here safe."

"And that's it? You're fine with that? You guys have just accepted that your lives must be lived together, while you always try to keep Machara locked away? What happens when Nicol dies? Do you continue guarding this place? What happens when all of you die?"

His tone was calm, and accepting. "The Eight will always be replaced with new men. It's the reason that even now we are searching for a man with magic that can replace Calder. And while Nicol's death is hopefully something none of us have to deal with for many, many years, it will change nothing. Machara will still be a threat that we can never allow to be released."

I couldn't wrap my mind around how all of them could be so docile about it. Their commitment to one another and to the Isle was noble, but it took away so much of their freedom.

"And you're okay with that? You have always been so independent, Marcus. You loved Boston, loved your friends and your job, and your family. You're really okay with spending your life here, dedicating it to this cause?"

"No, in all honesty, I'm not. And I think all of the men hope someday we will find a way to truly defeat her, but we all have to find a way to have some peace in our lives even if we don't." He paused. "And you're wrong about Boston. I put on a good face. While I loved my job, I was floundering in it. I wouldn't have been able to survive doing it another year. And as for my friends, my best one is here. Now, thanks to you, my family is, too. So, I'm okay. I'm still adjusting, but I really am okay."

I frowned as my frustration grew. There was a soft push against the cracked door, and I turned to see Mr. Crinkles saunter into the room. I ran across and snatched him up as I smothered him with kisses.

"There you are." Now that Mr. Crinkles had a whole castle to explore, it seemed like I saw a lot less of him.

Marcus smiled as Mr. Crinkles began to purr. "Look, I don't want to bullshit you. I'm not sure this is the life I would've chosen for myself, but it is what it is."

I looked up into his eyes, and a sort of dogged determination flared up inside me. I knew what it was like to have things you *couldn't* change. I would never grow my arm back. I couldn't go back to my life before the fire. I couldn't change what it meant for my life now, having to live without a part of myself. If Machara's hold on them was something these men *could* change, and I knew that it was, it made my blood boil to think that they weren't doing anything about it.

But they didn't know what I knew. Once they did, surely they would be on board, as well.

"Do you guys have some books around here? A library or anything? Don't all old castles have a good library?"

He laughed. "I think that assumption has come from one too many viewings of Beauty and the Beast, but yes, there is a library."

"Can I use it?"

He reached out to pull me into another hug. "Of course, you can use it."

It pleased me to see that Marcus had at least settled in to feeling at home here.

"Thank you. I've got something I need to take care of first, but if anyone can't find me later, that's where I'll be."

Dusk would be here soon.

It was time for me to meet Freya.

CHAPTER 28

That night just after dusk, before Nicol made his nightly trek down to the garden to spend the night with Freya, I went down to meet the ghostly woman I'd heard so much about.

It startled me when I saw her. While intellectually, I knew she would simply appear once the sun dropped into the sky—it was still shocking to witness. She was stunning. Translucent and bright, her long dark hair fell loosely around her waist, and her eyes were the darkest I'd ever seen. If not for her smile, she would've been rather frightening.

"I can see the resemblance between ye and yer sister. I'm verra fond of her."

I smiled. I couldn't help but stare at her, my eyes wandering up and down the length of her body. "I'm fond of her too. It's so nice to meet you."

"Come and sit, lass. Nicol willna be down for awhile still."

I followed her over to a small garden bench and together we sat down.

"Does he come even on nights like this? Even when it's freezing and raining?"

She nodded a little sadly. "He does. Despite my insistence that he needn't do so, he comes each and every night."

"He loves you."

"And I him. How do ye find the castle?"

I glanced up at the tall, foreboding fortress and then turned my gaze to the garden surrounding me. It had long since withered and died.

"The people are wonderful."

Freya laughed. "Ye long for more beauty just as I do, aye?"

"Why haven't they tended to this garden for you? Made it a place that is at least pleasing to be when you're here?"

"I doona believe it has occurred to them. Truly, there is no need. I couldna smell the flowers or feel the warmth even if 'twas here."

I knew from my own experiences beautifying people's surroundings that the aesthetics of one's home holds so much more power than people realize.

"No, but you could see them. Sometimes that makes all the difference."

She looked past me to a long-since-withered bush of something that once bloomed, and I could see the sadness in her eyes.

"Mayhap ye are right." She paused and reached for my hand. While I could see her touching me, I could feel nothing. It made my heart ache all the way through. How painful it would be to be stripped of the ability to feel someone's skin against your own. "I've a feeling Machara's temper willna be the only thing that changes now that ye are here."

"Machara's temper?" I looked at Freya curiously.

"Aye. She's frightened. Her hold over me has bound us together, and she has never been as frightened as she is now."

That gave me a sense of hope. I'd been right to ignore her stinky request that we meet. Whether Maddock and Nicol believed it or not, I was a threat to Machara, but I was currently more concerned with the other ways Freya mentioned that I might change things.

"I have an idea. What happens to you during the daytime?"

She shrugged. "I simply doona exist. 'Tis as if I'm sleeping, though I never dream."

"So, if there are men building and banging things around out here, it won't disturb you?"

She shook her head. "Nay, lass, it willna disturb mye. Might I ask what ye have planned?"

"A garden wedding, and a place for you and Nicol to finally find some peace."

I could tell that Raudrich was intrigued by my idea. He had both arms crossed tightly against his chest, but his brows were furrowed as if he was thinking. The more he thought, the more he began to smile. "'Twould please her, I'm certain."

I nodded. "I think it would. When Laurel spoke of the wedding she always wanted—not that she spoke of it very often—she always said she dreamed of an outdoor wedding, which isn't really possible in Scotland with the way the weather has been lately. And I also know that with the way you guys have decorated this place—as in, not at all—it's going to be really difficult to beautify it enough to be wedding-worthy over the course of the next nine days.

"If you guys pulled together to do this, if you could find some way to make what I've sketched out here, whether it be with your hands or magic, then it would solve so many problems. Not only would Laurel have the most beautiful wedding ever, but Nicol would have a place to spend his nights where he can stay dry and warm. Plus, perhaps most importantly, Freya will have some color in her life again."

Raudrich paced the length of the room for the longest time as he held my sketch out in front of him. Finally, after I was certain I would doze off while waiting for him, he turned and spoke. "'Twas truly not so difficult to spell the walls to Nicol's room, and I have often worried that we shall wake one morning to find him frozen to death outside. 'Tis possible such work would drain us less than much of the magic we often use."

"I guess you could give it a test first."

"Aye, we can test our magic on a small piece of the cabins we are building for all of ye." He paused and then threw his hands up as if he'd just had an idea. "I know how we can surprise both Laurel and Nicol."

"Oh yeah? How?"

"I know of a dressmaker on the mainland who could make Laurel the most beautiful dress. If I tell Laurel that we mean to finish the cabins with magic...'twould be a lie, o'course, but a worthy one, then mayhap she will agree to let Nicol take her there, seeing as he has no magic with which to help us."

I nodded excitedly. "That's perfect! What if the magic turns out to be too draining?"

Raudrich was too excited to back down from this idea now. He was all in.

"Then we will gather every able-bodied man on the Isle, and we shall build it by hand."

CHAPTER 29

*B*y the time Raudrich and I finished making the plans for our big surprise, it was too late for me to go to the library to do any research. So, I went to bed, got a few hours of shut-eye, and got up with the sun to head to the library.

I was shocked to see Maddock inside, sitting at a large table with three huge books spread out before him.

He was so engrossed in the material that he neither heard nor saw me when I walked in.

"Good morning. What are you working on?"

He jumped at the sound of my voice, and when he looked up, I could see that once again, he'd gotten very little sleep.

"Good morning, lass. Ye are the first person to ever come in here while I've been inside."

There was a large seat on the opposite side of the table, and I moved to join him.

"How often do you come in here?"

"Hardly ever before Laurel arrived."

I laughed. "Has her love of writing inspired a love of reading in you?"

"Not exactly. But her presence here on the Isle has made me question beliefs I once thought immovable."

"Such as?"

"For years I believed that our duty to this Isle was one that would last a lifetime, and for much of my life, I dinna mind it. But then yer sister arrived, and with wit and courage alone upended Machara's plans. It has made me wonder if mayhap we havena tried hard enough to rid ourselves of her."

I crossed my one arm over my chest and leaned back in the chair.

"I thought you said that mortal women could have no power over Machara."

He sighed and gave me a little grin. "Nicol is the last person I would wish to discuss any of this with. While he must be alerted to dangers, 'twould be cruel to give him hope until I have something truthful to tell him."

It made me much less concerned for the sanity of the members of The Eight to know that at least one of them wasn't content with living his entire life under Machara's thumb. It also made me wonder if since we both wanted the same thing, he might be more likely to help me.

I still believed that Brachan was somehow related to Nicol, but I was no closer to knowing how than when I arrived at the castle. The day after my intimate encounter with Maddock, I'd tried to broach the subject with Laurel, but she'd shut me down quickly—not that I could blame her. Until the wedding, she didn't want to speak or think about the evil faerie that had nearly killed her and the man she loved. After weeks of being on edge, she just wanted a short time of peace.

"Maddock?"

He placed his finger on the text to hold his place and looked up at me. "Aye, lass?"

"She can be defeated, but if she is, it won't be because of The Eight."

With his eyes still on me, he closed the book in front of him and leaned forward on the desk. "How could ye possibly know that, Kate?"

"I told you before. I've read about you guys. I did a lot of research in the days and weeks before coming here."

For the next several hours, I told Maddock everything I knew. He listened patiently, his eyes widening and narrowing at varying intervals. When I finished, he let out a big breath and shook his head. "We are all fools. Why dinna we seek more answers? Why did we all settle in and accept our lot here?"

"You're not fools. It's just...it's easy to get comfortable. Once you are, it's really difficult to change. Trust me. I should know."

"Lass..."

I cut him off. I'd not meant for my admission to lead to a conversation about us, and I wasn't sure I could take him telling me once again that he had no intention of pursuing anything else with me. Maddock was right. Of course, I wanted him. I wanted him so badly that each night falling asleep in his bed, without him there, was a dreadful sort of torture. I just didn't know how to change things now that he seemed so set on just being friends.

"There's something else. You remember the healer from the village? Brachan? I think he must be related to Nicol. Is that possible? They look so much alike."

Maddock smiled. "O'course ye noticed. There is no doubt in my mind the lad is related to Nicol."

"Could it be his cousin, or perhaps a nephew?"

"No, lass. If Brachan is not Nicol's son, then I shall never trust my own eyes again."

His son. Some small part of my mind had wondered, but it was a thought I'd dismissed quickly. I knew he bore no children with Freya. Was it possible that Brachan was half-fae? Could he be one of the children Nicol bore with Machara? Had she truly not killed them all?

Maddock could guess the questions running through my mind.

"I doona know, lass. I tried to tell Nicol about the lad the day we arrived, but he wouldna hear it. He ordered me to say nothing of it until after the wedding."

It seemed everyone in the castle, save Maddock and me, was on the same page in regard to Machara.

"Laurel dismissed me, as well, when I tried to ask her about it. So, what do we do?"

"For now, we read to see if we can learn more, but we listen to everyone's wishes and do nothing until after Laurel and Raudrich are wed."

"What then?"

"Then I take ye to Machara whether ye wish to see her or not. From everything ye've told me, 'tis ye that will have to face her, and we need to know if Brachan is part of her plan to harm ye and break free. If he is, then I shall find the lad and kill him."

"Maddock." A sudden rush of defensiveness sprang up inside me. Brachan had saved my life, not harmed me. "What if Brachan doesn't even know who he is? I really think he's innocent in all this."

"He knows, or at least the woman who raised him does. She dinna care for it when I brought up how much he resembled Nicol. How can ye assume he's innocent? Ye doona know him."

"I know that he saved my life. Maddock, he was kind. I just didn't get that sort of read from him."

"Regardless, lass, I doona want him near ye." He stood and flattened his palm against the top of the desk. "For now, I must put all of this aside. It seems I should thank ye for the hard work we must put in today."

I grinned guiltily. "It's going to be wonderful when it's finished."

"Aye, lass, 'tis. Let us send Nicol and Laurel away so we may set to work."

CHAPTER 30

ine Days Later

audrich over-delivered. Seriously over-delivered. While all of the men pooled their magic to bring up the glass walls, the intricate doorway, the arched glass ceiling, and all the plants and flowers, he'd been the perfectionist among them, making certain that my vision was executed to a T.

Laurel and Nicol's trip to the mainland took much longer than anyone expected, but it turned out for the best. It allowed me to make sure everything was perfect on the inside after they finished with the actual structure.

By the time everything was finished, it was better than I'd drawn it and far more impressive than I ever imagined.

It didn't fit with the rest of the castle, but in time, once I bested Machara in whatever way I was meant to, I would continue to work on the castle. Eventually, everything would be as beautiful as this space was now.

The conservatory was a sanctuary of greenery and warmth. The old fountain was now restored, and the most delightful trickle of water could be heard from anywhere inside.

Freya loved it. Each night when she appeared, she delighted in the progress that had been made during the day.

Laurel and Nicol were going to freak.

In an effort to keep myself distracted from the anticipation of Laurel and Nicol's return later that day, I talked Harry—he was on breakfast duty—into taking me down to the village for a second breakfast of sorts. I couldn't take another meal of fish, and I thought the outing might settle my jitters.

---

*T*here were parts of the Isle that looked familiar to him, but only in the half-hazy way that childhood memories often are. No one would know who he was. None there knew him, and that was for the best.

Brachan only hoped that his mother's belief in him was justified—that he would be able to resist the pull of Machara and that one day he would learn how to rid himself of the evil brewing inside him.

He directed his horse toward the smell of cooked food. While he knew his wisest course of action would be to stay away from the locals, he couldn't deny himself a decent meal after such a cold and miserable journey.

The inside of the tavern was warm and inviting, and to his delight, it was for the most part empty. Only one person sat at the bar and he knew immediately who she was.

Kate.

Perhaps some loving deity had blessed his journey to the Isle, after all. It gave him hope that everything would turn out okay.

*T*he eggs were delicious, all the more so because they effectively rid my mouth of the taste of fish.

Harry and I had eaten together in silence, and when I gave him my word that I would not wander off, he stepped out back to visit with the owner of the tavern.

I heard the door open but thought nothing of it as I continued to eat away at the half-dozen eggs that lay on my plate. It was only when I heard his voice that I stilled. I knew it was Brachan from his first word.

"Kate, 'tis lovely to see ye again."

My first instinct was to turn around and hug his neck. I was grateful for what he'd done for me, and I'd liked him right away. But instead, as I heard Harry's voice bellow from the back—a sign he was ending his conversation and would be on his way back in here soon—I panicked, spun around, grabbed his hand, and quickly ushered him outside without saying a word.

I didn't stop until we were hidden beside the building. When I finally looked up into his face, his eyes were filled with concern.

"What is the matter, lass? Are ye with someone?"

"Yes, and Harry can't see you. He will notice the same thing that Maddock and I did. You look just like Nicol."

He sighed. "Ye know I am his son?"

Nodding, I watched him carefully. "I do now." He didn't appear to be someone with some evil plan to destroy anyone. "Did you know that you were Nicol's son?"

"I only learned who my father was the day after I healed ye, lass."

"And what of your mother? Do you know who she is?" It was a personal question to ask him, but I needed to know.

177

"My mother is the woman who raised me. If ye mean to ask who gave birth to me, I believe ye already know."

"Machara."

He ground his teeth as he nodded. "I only just learned that, as well. I can feel her calling me to her, lass. 'Tis as if some evil has invaded my mind, and every day it is harder to fight."

Brachan wanted no part of whatever evil plan Machara was brewing up, of that I was certain.

I reached for his hand. "Brachan, you should come with me back to the castle. Tell the men everything you just told me. They can help think of a way to free you from her. They will realize that you cannot help who your birth mother is."

Panic flashed through his eyes as he pulled away from my grip. "No, lass. Speak to the men, I will, but I canna do so just yet. I need some time here to think of what I will say. I...I doona know how to meet my father. He hated me. He thought me dead, and he was glad of it. Please, Kate, I beg ye. Doona tell them that I am here. Give me some time—a day, mayhap two—to gather the strength I need."

I cringed at the thought, and it pained me to know that it was true. But that was only because Nicol didn't know. He didn't realize that his children with Machara weren't monsters. If he'd known, he wouldn't have felt as he did, and he surely wouldn't feel that way once he saw the man Brachan had become.

Although Maddock would consider it a betrayal if he found out I knew Brachan was on the Isle and didn't tell him, I knew that he would drag Brachan in front of Nicol the first moment he saw him, and I could understand Brachan's need to prepare for such an introduction.

"Okay. I won't say anything, I promise."

"Thank ye, lass." He bent and pulled me into a hug. "Best ye go. Harry is on his way inside. I shall see ye again soon."

He turned and ran away from the tavern, and I made it to my seat just as Harry entered the room.

CHAPTER 31

"Where are you two leading us?"

Laurel's voice was excited, and she gripped my hand tightly as I guided her through the doors of the garden.

With the rest of the men already waiting inside the garden to see their reactions, Raudrich and I apprehended Laurel and Nicol the moment their horses reached the gate leading up to the castle. We couldn't risk them seeing the new structure as they rode up the hill, so we forced them to walk up blindfolded, with only us to guide them.

"I wish ye would release me, Raudrich. I doona care for surprises."

"Only a few more steps. Doona worry, ye have my word that ye will enjoy this surprise."

Once they were both inside, we steadied them on their feet and made our way to stand in front of them before removing the blindfolds. We both wanted to see their faces when they saw the garden for the first time.

"Okay, guys, you ready?"

181

I looked over at Raudrich for approval, and together we uncovered their eyes and stepped quickly away.

It took them a moment to take everything in. As tightly as we'd bound their eyes, I'm certain they'd been blinded when first exposed to the light. But then, as everything began to register, their reactions couldn't have been better.

Nicol nearly fell, but Paton was there in an instant to see him seated on one of the garden's many stone benches. Silent tears ran down his cheeks as he took everything in.

Laurel's mouth fell open as she looked at me for confirmation. "Is this...how did you guys?"

"Yes, it's the garden. The guys did everything. They pooled their magic and worked on it every day since you two left. We wanted to surprise both of you. We thought this would be the perfect spot for your wedding tomorrow, and we thought this would be a gift that Nicol and Freya could enjoy each and every night."

For the first time since seeing the space, Nicol spoke, his voice choked with tears. "Has Freya...has she seen it?"

"Aye, we made certain all designs were approved by her. It will, after all, be her home."

Nicol broke down into a full-on sob, cradling his face in his hands as Paton wrapped his arm over his shoulder.

"Do ye like it, Nicol?"

He lifted his head, and the sight of him crying made me start to blubber, as well.

"Like it? I doona know if I've ever been so happy. The thoughtfulness of all of ye..." He paused as another sob overtook him. "I doona...I doona ever think I've been so overwhelmed."

The men gathered around Nicol, each of them embracing in a big group hug that made me wish more than anything that I had a camera.

As I looked on, Laurel came up behind me and wrapped her arms around me. "This is the perfect wedding gift, Kate."

I faced her and took her hand. "I'm glad you like it. Now, let's go and finish up all of the last minute stuff so we can get you married."

---

*L*aurel wasn't the only one that got a surprise before the wedding. Minutes before the ceremony was meant to start, as residents of the Isle found their seats in the garden, I left Laurel in her bedchamber with our mother so that I could run downstairs to make certain everything was ready for her entrance. As I neared the castle doors, some unexpected guests arrived—Sydney and her husband, Gillian and Orick, and Callum's brother, Griffith, walked in looking nothing like they'd just spent days on the road.

I quickly ran over to hug Sydney. "How did you get here? Oh my gosh, Raudrich is going to be thrilled to see you, Sydney."

She smiled. "Is he..." She pointed outside.

"Yes, he's already at the front, waiting for his bride."

Sydney nodded as if that was what she'd expected. "Okay, we will slip in and sit in the back. I'll talk to him after."

"You guys didn't ride here, did you? I thought you didn't want to travel on account of the baby."

"We decided to make the trip to Morna's house via car and have her send us back here from there. She assured me the baby would be in no danger."

The sun had long since dipped, and the stars were out in full show. It was time for the wedding to begin.

"Okay, well, David is ushering everyone to their seats, so go on in. I'm so pleased that you all are here."

With none of his immediate family remaining, it would mean the world to Raudrich that Sydney had come. Ever since he'd kidnapped her to save her life (long story) several years ago, they'd been the best of friends.

After making certain the garden looked perfect, I went to retrieve Mom and Laurel. Laurel had never looked more radiant, and I started to cry the moment I saw her.

"Oh my God, Laurel. You're stunning."

She looked down at her gown a little self-consciously. "Do you think so?"

"I know so. Are you ready to do this?"

"I've never been so ready for anything in my life."

Together, with my mom on one side of Laurel and me on the other, we made our way down to the garden.

Raudrich's expression when he saw Laurel was one I knew I would remember for the rest of my life.

---

*F*ollowing the ceremony, we quickly cleared out the chairs and had the reception out there as well. It was the perfect setting, and something about the beauty of the place seemed to make people a little less rowdy than I suspected they would have been had we moved everyone inside the castle.

There was ale, music, dancing, and laughter, and Laurel and Raudrich seemed to love every minute of it.

As the sister of the bride, I felt some responsibility to make certain everything was going smoothly, so rather than enjoy the festivities myself, I continually made my way around the garden checking on things and making small talk.

An hour or so into the reception, Marcus came up and gave my wrist a gentle tug. "Come and dance with me, Kate.

Everything is fine. There's no need for you to wear yourself out running around."

I smiled and allowed him to pull me into the area surrounding the fountain where people were dancing.

"Do you know how to dance these Scottish dances, Marcus?"

He shook his head and laughed. "Not at all. I'll just hold you and we can sway back and forth a bit."

"Sounds perfect."

We danced with one another in silence for a moment, and I lost myself in thought until Marcus bent down to whisper in my ear, "Penny for your thoughts?"

"I was just thinking about Raudrich. Did you see the way he looked at Laurel? Do you think I'll ever find someone to look at me that same way?"

He pulled back a little so he could look down at my face. "You're kidding, right?" When I said nothing, he continued. "Kate, you do have someone who looks at you like that. I was standing directly across from Maddock on Laurel's side of the aisle, and the look on Maddock's face..." He hesitated and gave me a grin. "It would have been easy to mistake him for the groom, but he wasn't looking at Laurel."

"No." I shook my head, quickly dismissing it. "You're mistaken, Marcus. He might have been attracted to me, but I did a really good job of ruining that a few days ago."

"Kate." He stopped dancing and pulled me over to one of the many walkways scattered throughout the garden. "You haven't ruined anything yet, but as your friend, I'm going to be totally honest with you. For a very long time, none of the men here believed that romantic relationships were something available to them. Raudrich finding love with Laurel changed that. They now see love as a possibility, and there's not a one of them that's not eager for it."

"Even you?" I interrupted him in a veiled attempt to redirect the conversation. It didn't work.

"Yes, Kate. Even me. Listen, Maddock wants *you*. He's crazy about *you*. But he's not going to waste his time on someone who is too scared to take a chance on him. Look at him." He moved behind me and crouched down to direct my attention where he pointed.

Maddock stood next to the fountain with a mug of ale in his hand as he laughed and visited with a group of men from the village.

"I see him. So?"

He changed the direction of his finger and pointed to three different women standing in different locations throughout the garden.

"Now take a good long look at each of those women, Kate. Look at the way they're looking at him. I've no doubt that women have always looked at him that way, but when he didn't think love was an option, he never took notice. Now that he does, how long do you think it will be before he sees their interest in him?" He paused and turned me toward him. "He doesn't want those women, Kate. He wants you. But for a man who's been alone as long as he has, it might seem more tempting to settle than to end up all alone."

The thought of Maddock with any of those women caused jealousy to run through me hot and fast.

"So, what are you saying?"

He dropped his hands from my shoulders and stepped back as he shook his head. "Do you want him, Kate? And don't you dare give me the same bullshit non-answer I'm sure you would give everyone else."

"Marcus, I am trying. I do..." Marcus' tone was making me

emotional. He'd never spoken to me so harshly before. "I do want him. I just…"

"Stop, Kate." He interrupted me and his tone softened just a bit. "Trying isn't good enough. You either decide that you want him, or you don't. Be all in or be all out. There is no trying. Now." He bobbed his head in the direction behind me. "I'll lead by example and push through some of my own fear, okay? There's a woman over there that I've been wanting to speak to all night. I think she's from Raudrich's old clan. I'm so nervous I could vomit, but guess what, Kate, I'm going to do it anyway. It's time for you to do the same."

CHAPTER 32

*M*arcus' words seemed to get to me in a way that nobody else's had been able to. He'd said basically the same thing my therapist, my mother, and Laurel had been hinting at for weeks, but there was something about hearing it from him—someone who'd only ever been ridiculously kind to me—that made me realize just how stupid I had become. I didn't allow myself to indulge in avoidance in any other area of my life—not my work, not my physical recovery. So why was I doing it with my love life?

Yes, the thought of falling for Maddock terrified me. But, so what? If the fire hadn't killed me, there was no way in hell a little fear was going to make me keel over.

I took a moment to hug Laurel and Raudrich—to wish them well on their honeymoon, then I slipped away to Maddock's room to prepare myself for what I knew I needed to do.

Once there, I sank to the floor in front of the one piece of mirrored glass in the room and closed my eyes so I could get really, really quiet. It didn't take long before my mind started to rebel, before it started to throw up all sorts of thoughts meant to keep me from feeling, but I fought against them. As every buried emotion came up, I allowed myself to feel it.

I don't know how long I sat there—crying, screaming, cackling like a weirdo—while I worked through a year's worth of emotions over the course of a few hours.

All I know is that when I was done, something inside me was free. I was ready to move on from this problem so I would be ready for the next. But in the meantime, while things were good, I would enjoy it. I was tired of ruining blessings by hanging onto the rotten stuff I'd already been through.

By the time I was ready to go in search of Maddock, the party outside had quieted down. Raudrich and Laurel had already left for the small inn near the tavern where they would spend their first night as husband and wife before continuing on to the Scottish mainland where they would have their honeymoon. Most of the guests were leaving, and Paton was seeing Sydney and her crew to various bedchambers throughout the castle. It looked like all of the members of The Eight would be sleeping in the unfinished cabins they'd been working on for weeks.

"Ye did well, lass. They couldna have asked for a more beautiful wedding and all of that is due to ye." His voice came from behind me on the stairwell and I smiled as I turned to face him.

"I think you all are allowed to take quite a bit of credit, as well. You're the ones who did all of the hard work. I just drew up the plans."

"Lass, 'tis an idea that should've occurred to us long ago, but we are all too selfish to have thought of it. I canna fathom that we allowed Nicol to spend every night in the cold outdoors for so long."

"And what about all of you? With all of the guests being

shown to your rooms, will you be forced to sleep in the roofless cottages out back?"

He shook his head, and I stepped down two steps so I would be even with him.

"No, lass. Nicol has invited us to make camp in the garden. So, we will sleep with a view of the stars, but we shall be protected from the wind.

It was now or never. If I didn't tell him now while my courage was up after my cathartic emotional cleansing, I would never to it.

"Maddock, I need to tell you something."

He looked concerned. "Aye, lass? Have ye learned something else? Is it about Machara?"

"No. It has nothing to do with any of that." There were still a few people milling around the castle, and the last thing I wanted was for anyone else to hear my confession. "Can we go someplace where we can be alone?"

"O'course, lass. Do ye want to go to my bedchamber? 'Tis yers now anyway, and it may be the only place in the castle where we are sure to be able to speak alone."

Nodding, I moved past him and headed in that direction. I had no plan for what I meant to say to him, and I had every expectation that Marcus was wrong—that I was too late and that Maddock wouldn't be interested in taking a risk on me again. Still, I knew I would kick myself forever if I didn't try. And the thought of me spending the rest of my life in this castle, having to watch Maddock be with whoever he ended up with, was more terrifying than making myself vulnerable to him now.

The words spilled out of me the moment he closed the door after we entered his bedchamber. "I don't want to be your friend, Maddock."

"What, lass?"

My breath shaky and my voice soft, I faced him. "I don't want to be your friend. I've enough of those. I'm sorry I was so scared before. Maddock I...I'll understand if you don't want me anymore, if my initial rejection was enough to turn you off, but I needed you to know. You were right. Of course, you were right. I want you so much, it's all I can think about. And..."

He was on me in an instant. His mouth claiming mine with such intensity that it was nearly painful. I could taste the ale he'd had at the wedding still on his tongue.

"Kate." His voice was ragged and low, and his teeth grazed against my lips as he spoke. "Do ye truly believe I ever had any interest in being yer friend? If 'twas all ye could give me, I would take it, but Kate, every time I look at ye, I have to think of something horrid just to keep from growing hard from my need of ye. I've never wanted anything in my life more than I want ye." He pulled away from me just long enough to look into my eyes. "Are ye sure of this? Ye doona mean to change yer mind? Pulling away from yer bare breasts was hard enough the first time. I doona know if I have the strength to stop once again."

Clothes had never felt so restrictive. My entire body ached with desire. I wasn't sure he could ever fill me enough to satisfy my need for him.

"I'm sure. I promise I won't change my mind. Please, Maddock. Take me to your bed."

His response came in the form of an animalistic groan. At once, his hands were at my back, untying my laces so he could remove my dress.

There was a sudden meow from the bed, and I started to laugh as Maddock's hands stilled.

"I canna tup ye with him watching, lass. The sounds I intend to draw from ye will frighten him, and I doona wish to have my eyes clawed out by yer wee protector."

He'd only begun to work on my laces so I was still completely dressed.

"Take off your kilt and lay down on the bed, Maddock. I'll take him to the garden where he can sleep with the other men tonight. I'll be back in just a moment."

I ran faster than I'd ever run in my life, and I continually had to hold Mr. Crinkles away from me as he tried to swat at me in his wish to be set down. I didn't even say anything to the men as I opened the door to the garden and gently tossed Crink inside. I knew he would be fine.

When I returned to his room, he'd done as I asked. The sight of him propped up on the bed entirely naked caused the breath to lodge in my throat. Immediately my cheeks flushed red.

I'd seen his chest that night in Cagair Castle, but seeing that was quite different from seeing the whole specimen at once. Every muscle in his body was cut from hard work and clean food. He looked like a statue you might see in Italy, although thankfully he didn't have the same scrawny manhood that so many ancient statues seemed to possess. One look at his erection and I realized quickly that my worry of being unable to get my fill of him was misplaced.

"Holy crap, Maddock. That's...you're..."

He laughed and waved me toward the bed. "It pleases me that ye approve, lass. Now get over here so that I may see ye, as well."

I sat at the edge of the bed as he worked my laces. This gown had more than most. It was especially for Laurel's wedding and was more complex than the simple gowns I'd worn most days since arriving in this time.

"Damn these laces, lass. Do ye mind if I slice them open with my sword?"

Laughing, I reached behind my back seeking one of his hands. "Please, don't. This was Freya's. It's too beautiful to ruin."

"Ach, fine, but it may be sunrise before I get ye out of it." He continued to pull at the strings as he bent to nibble at my neck. "Lass, I know that the first time is often frightening. I doona want ye to be scared. I'll be gentle with ye. I'll take my time."

I snorted, cutting him off. "Maddock, you do remember Dillon, right?"

He groaned and lay his forehead on my shoulder. "Why would ye ever bring him up in this moment, lass?"

"You're not under the assumption that I'm a virgin, are you?"

His hands stilled on my lower back as he raised his head. "Are ye not, lass?"

"No." His assumption didn't anger me. I supposed in his time, many women would be. "Women in my time rarely are by my age. It doesn't bother you, does it?"

His fingers resumed their movement on my laces, and I exhaled a breath I'd not know I'd held.

"All that bothers me is the thought of Dillon's hands anywhere on ye, lass. In truth, 'tis better this way. It means I can truly have my way with ye."

My gown was now undone, and I stood and shimmied my shoulders and let the dress fall to the floor.

"Or I can have my way with you. Lay back, buster."

Maddock growled as he lay back on the bed. "Do ye mean to kill me, lass? Ye canna expect me to lie here while ye stand there like that..."

I faced him, and his breath became ragged as his eyes raked over my naked body. I wasn't self-conscious in front of Maddock. He'd already shown me so many times before—whether it was the way he'd warmed my arms when I was cold, or the way he'd held me close while we rode Stella to the Isle—that my amputation meant nothing to him. And there was nothing but need and desire in his gaze as he devoured me with his eyes.

"I canna stand it a moment longer, lass. I need to be inside ye."

My arm prevented me from crawling over to him on the bed. Instead, I sat and scooted over to him, leaning in to kiss him as my breasts brushed against his chest. He understood what was needed, and his hands moved to my waist to lift me just enough so I could straddle him.

I trailed kisses down his chest. As I reached his manhood, I lifted up on my knees so I could lower myself onto him.

We came together smoothly, and both of us cried out as he filled me.

"Kate, ye must move, lass. I canna bear it."

I moved slowly, torturing him just a little, and I reveled in the effect each little movement of my hips had on him. When I finally picked up speed and the sensation built within me, he couldn't stand it any longer. Lifting himself, he grabbed my waist, flipped me over, and pinned me beneath him as our bodies ground together. He drove into me over and over as his lips tasted and explored my body.

We reached completion together, and it was only the first of many times we enjoyed each other that night.

It was fine with me if the sun never rose again. It would mean that every minute in the darkness with him would go on forever—minutes I was growing increasingly sure that I would never grow tired of.

CHAPTER 33

We slept until afternoon the next day, and while we were both still a little high on each other, reality set in quickly. Laurel and Raudrich's wedding was now over. It was time for Maddock to speak to Nicol about Brachan, and I needed to finally see Machara for myself so we could try to get a read on her intentions.

"I know we've much to do, but I am famished, lass."

My stomach was growling, as well, and now that I didn't have raging sex hormones clouding my judgment, I was beginning to feel a little guilty for kicking Mr. Crinkles out of the room.

"I am too. Why don't you go and speak with Nicol now? We slept for over half the day, so I'm sure he's already awake from his morning slumber. You're not going to feel better about anything until you get that off your chest. I'll check on Crink and try to win him back by finding him some fish and get some food for us, as well. Meet here in a little while?"

I'd slept on my side while Maddock spooned me, and the entire night he'd held onto one of my breasts as we slept. His hand was still there.

"Aye, ye are right. I must speak to Nicol before we plan anything else. It willna take long. Nicol is always a man of verra few words."

"Okay, then. You're going to have to let go of me first in order to get dressed."

"Ach, lass. I doona ever want to let go of ye."

I squirmed away from him so I could roll off the bed. Otherwise, I was afraid we would be there all day.

"Too bad. Get up, sleepy head. It's a big day. One that we can't afford to waste."

He was still procrastinating when I walked out the door to get us food.

———

*M*addock was still gone when I made it back to the room with Mr. Crinkles draped over my arm and Paton hot on my heels with a tray of bread and cheese—no fish —for me and Maddock.

"I knew the only reason Maddock wouldna let me escort ye back when ye fell ill was because he fancied ye."

"You'll keep it a secret, won't you, Paton?"

He set the tray of food down carefully then doubled over with laughter. "Kate, lass, everyone in the castle has been awake since dawn, but not a one of us saw either of ye until moments ago. There is no secret for me to keep. Everyone knows."

That should've been obvious to me, but it hadn't crossed my mind. "Even my mother?"

Paton crinkled up his nose. "Aye, and wouldna ye know it, she still likes Maddock better than me. He is the one tuppin' her daughter, yet for some reason, I'm the one she still canna stand."

"She likes you, Paton. That's the only reason she gives you

198

such a hard time. It's not like you don't ask for it. You annoy her on purpose because you like getting a reaction from her."

He shrugged as Maddock appeared in the doorway. "Mayhap so. It looks as if yer lover has returned. I'll leave the two of ye alone."

Maddock punched his arm as he walked by. "Why doona ye have a little more respect than that, Paton? Lover sounds as if we are doing something untoward."

Paton laughed and blocked another swat from Maddock's hand. "Some would say ye are."

Maddock ground his teeth. "Get out, Paton."

I could hear Paton's laughter echoing down the hallway long after Maddock closed the door in his face.

I waited until Maddock was seated at the small table where I'd situated our food to ask him about his conversation with Nicol. "So...how did it go?"

Maddock sighed and looked down at the piece of cheese he held in his hand. "Nicol is beside himself. There is no doubt that the child is Machara's. He has only ever been with her and Freya. While I've my own suspicions of Brachan, I've no desire to pass judgement before we've spoken to the lad. But if he plans to work with Machara, I shall have no qualms about killing him. Nicol, however, wishes to kill him on sight."

"What?" Horror surged through my body. "Why? Why would he want to do that to his own son?"

"For years, Nicol told himself that his children with Machara were monsters. 'Twas the only way he could keep from losing himself to guilt and despair at their murders. If he allows himself to believe that Brachan might be different, then he must accept that all the others were, as well."

"Do you think he will feel that way once he meets him?"

"No. I think when Nicol sees his own eyes looking back at

him, it will send him into a grief that will be hard to come out of —one that he will have to work through in his own time."

Maddock still didn't know that Brachan was already on the Isle. He needed to know so he could protect Brachan long enough for Nicol to truly see him, but I couldn't bring myself to break my promise to the man who'd saved my life.

"What does Nicol wish to do?"

"He wishes to meet with everyone at dusk. He will tell the others what I have revealed to him. Together, we will decide how best to go and search for Nicol's son. Until then, I would like to eat and mayhap take ye to my bed once more, for I suspect that after Nicol speaks with us, I will be sent away to look for Brachan since I've seen him before. I need all the memories of being with ye I can get to keep me sane while I'm away from ye."

I needed to find Brachan. I needed to tell him that the men would go looking for him if he didn't make himself known soon, but I couldn't tell Maddock that, and I certainly wasn't opposed to being taken to his bed one more time.

"Do you intend to keep me in your bed until dusk? If we keep it up at the rate we went last night, we are both going to be so sore, we won't be able to move."

He lifted one brow mischievously. "I like the thought of that, but alas, no. 'Tis time for ye to meet Machara, but first..." He threw the cheese down, lifted me from the chair, and carried me to the bed. "I shall make love to ye once more."

CHAPTER 34

The greenish light that filled Machara's dungeon was enough to invoke fear in even the most courageous of people. The terror I felt while descending the stairs to the prison was so acute, I wasn't sure I would've been able to move if not for Maddock's reassuring hand on my back, slowly pushing me downward.

As we neared the last step, he leaned down to whisper in my ear, "Doona breathe through yer nose, lass. It makes it worse. And doona let her see how frightened ye are."

I already knew that much. The last thing I would ever let Machara see was that I was frightened of her. That was exactly why I moved down so slowly—I needed every last step to gather my courage.

She spoke before she even saw us, and her tone was as frightening and filled with malice as one would expect. "Ah, the new one has finally gathered the courage to come and see me."

At the end of the stairs, we stepped in front of her cell, and I saw her for the first time.

I'm not sure what I expected, but every part of her was just a little bit *more* than what I imagined. She was taller, thinner, and her nails came to creepy long points that made me want to gag. Her neck was long and gorgeous, and her eyes were a color entirely inhuman in nature.

Maddock spoke before I had the chance. "It had nothing to do with courage, Machara. She had no interest in seeing ye."

"Bollocks. I can smell the fear on her."

I could feel that Maddock meant to speak again, and I hurried to step in front of him. I didn't appreciate either of them speaking about me as if I wasn't there.

"Maybe you're smelling your own stench, Machara. Fear wasn't what kept me away, it was disinterest. We've all been rather busy with the wedding. You remember my sister, don't you? She's the one you tried to kill, but she outwitted you so, so easily."

She hissed at the mention of my sister, and her face twisted into something that looked far more otherworldly than human, and it made me wonder just how capable she was of twisting her shape.

"'Tis true that I grew reckless in my haste to be free of this prison, but I willna make the same mistake again."

Maddock stepped between us, his temper short as he spoke to her. "Yer son, Machara. We have him."

I watched her eyes carefully, but they gave nothing away.

"Ye doona have him, but ye shall all know him soon enough."

He crossed his arms and kept his expression steady. "And just what do ye believe he will do to us?"

She smiled, and every hair on my body prickled uncomfortably. "He will help me destroy ye. 'Tis his destiny to do so. He will be powerless to resist my call."

Maddock grabbed my hand and pulled me away, not stopping until we were up the stairs and back inside Nicol's bedchamber.

"Why would she tell you that?"

"'Tis one of Machara's many flaws. She believes herself invincible, even after being bested over and over again. She doesna hide anything, for she believes it doesna matter if we know. But it does, lass. And now, I am inclined to agree with Nicol. We canna allow Brachan to live."

I had no time to sneak away to search for Brachan. I didn't even have time to come clean to Maddock about the fact that I'd seen him several days ago. By the time Maddock and I stepped out of Nicol's room, the men were gathering in the dining hall for their meeting with Nicol.

I was tortured over what to do. I couldn't allow them to sit around and make plans to kill an innocent man. I'd heard every word Machara said, but her words had done nothing to make me feel differently about him.

I'd seen the pained expression in Brachan's eyes. All of this was new to him, and he didn't want Machara inside his mind. If there was any way for him to resist her, Brachan would find it. The Eight just needed to give him the chance.

I didn't ask if I could attend. I simply took a seat in what I presumed was usually Raudrich's chair and ignored every surprised glance that passed my way.

Maddock, at least, understood why I was in attendance.

"Ignore them, lass. They doona yet know that this involves ye as much as anyone."

I decided my best course of action was to wait and see how the conversation panned out. Hopefully one of the other men would share my sentiment—that they couldn't plan to kill a man who'd yet to do anything wrong.

Nicol took the lead, but other than telling them that he'd learned one of his children with Machara still lived, he didn't say much and quickly passed the baton to Maddock, who filled the rest of the men in on everything else.

For much of Maddock's explanation, the men seemed to be in agreement with my point of view, but the moment Maddock told them what Machara had said, their minds swayed to Maddock's way of thinking.

Harry was the first to voice his concern. "We canna risk it. We all remember how Machara was able to control Calder, and he dinna have a drop of her blood within him. This man is of her blood."

I stood, realizing it no longer benefited Brachan for me to keep his secret.

"Wait just a minute, Harry. You guys have to judge this man for yourselves. Just because things played out with Calder one way, doesn't mean they will work the same way with Brachan. After all, Brachan is half Nicol's, and you know that must mean he has some goodness in him. I've spent more time with Brachan than anyone, and I truly don't believe him to be a threat."

Paton spoke up from across the table. "Time, lass? Ye were unconscious for most of the time he spent by yer side."

I glanced at Maddock nervously. He would be so angry, but it was time for me to tell all of them. "I saw him after I was awake, and he was nothing but kind. And I saw him the other day in the village."

As if my mention of him summoned him from the ether, the doors to the dining hall opened, and Brachan stepped inside.

CHAPTER 35

"Forgive me for intruding. I've powers that allowed me to see ye were gathered here. I thought it best to come before ye all at once."

Maddock, God bless him. Despite his claims after meeting Machara that he was ready to kill Brachan, even though I knew my confession had him feeling betrayed and angry, he stood and put himself between Brachan and the rest of the men.

"We must hear him out, lads. He dinna have to come here. He could have allowed us to search for him."

The rest of the men remained silent. As Maddock led Brachan over to the table, I glanced over to Nicol. He'd been standing, but he now sunk weakly back in his chair, his face going white. I could see his hand trembling from the other end of the table.

I couldn't imagine what he was thinking. A son he believed dead, a son he'd hated, one who looked just like him, was now standing before him. And like Maddock had suggested, it had to be difficult to deny Brachan's humanity when you listened to his voice and looked into his eyes.

Harry was the first one to speak after Maddock ushered Brachan over to my side. "If ye are not here to cause us harm, if ye doona mean to do Machara's bidding, then how do ye know us? Ye dinna grow up here on this Isle. We would've seen ye before now if ye had."

Before Brachan said anything, he turned to look at me and smiled. "Hello, lass. Thank ye for trying to keep my secret, and thank ye for standing up for me just now."

I smiled and gave him a small nod, but his words made my stomach turn over. If my confession hadn't been enough to make Maddock's blood boil, Brachan had certainly driven the point home now. I gave him a careful glance, but Maddock wouldn't meet my eye.

Brachan then turned his attention to the men and made his plea. "I have known for my entire life that the woman who raised me is not the woman who gave birth to me, but I only recently learned of my lineage. I assure ye, I wish I dinna know. It brought me no joy to learn that the lass who gave birth to me could be so evil, nor to know that my father believed me dead and was glad of it."

Nicol looked as if he might be ill at any moment, but he said nothing. I wasn't sure he was capable of it in this moment.

Brachan continued, "I was born with magic inside me—powerful magic that has allowed me to heal many. I have always used my powers for good, but as of late, I can feel them twisting inside me. I can feel Machara reaching out to me. I can feel her calling me to her.

"I am not here to help her, I swear to ye that. I am here to ask for yer help. Help in ridding me of the darkness that is beginning to overtake my mind. Help in severing any and all ties she may have on me."

For a long moment, no one said anything. One by one they

turned their gazes to Nicol as they looked toward their master for guidance.

Nicol cleared his throat and took a deep breath that caused some color to return to his cheeks. He planted both palms down on the table, and shakily pressed himself up until he was standing.

"Brachan, lad. Come with me. There is much we need to discuss, and I doona wish to have an audience."

———

*Y*e lied, lass. Ye knew where he was, and ye kept it from me. How long have ye known?" Maddock was screaming. The muscles in his jaw looked like they might break right through the skin of his cheek.

"I couldn't tell you, Maddock. I promised him."

"I doona give a damn if ye promised him, lass. I asked ye a question. How long have ye known he was here?"

I took a breath and closed my eyes. "Since the day before the wedding."

"For days, lass? Ye've known for days, and ye said nothing. After everything we shared together, how do ye ever expect me to trust ye again?"

"Hang on." I held up my palm to stop him, my own anger coming hot and fast. "Don't you dare pull that crap. How could you trust a woman that breaks her promises to friends? Brachan was frightened, Maddock. Clearly he had good reason to be. Both you, Nicol, and Harry were ready to kill him before we walked into that room. I trust him. I believe every word he said at that table. He needs your help, not your anger."

"Lass..."

"No." I cut him off, opened the door to his bedroom and

gestured with my hand for him to leave. "I'm not going to listen to you scream at me. Get out and cool off. I'm sorry if you feel betrayed, but I did the right thing. I don't regret my decision. We can talk about this later."

He looked a bit like a dog with his tail between his legs when he left.

---

*W*as she right? Was it wrong of him to be angry with her? It was true that his first reaction to Machara's words was to wish Brachan dead, but he truly wouldna have harmed the lad without determining his intentions first. Would he?

He shouldn't have yelled at her, he knew that much was true. She was right to send him from the room. The way she'd chided him, the way she'd stood up for herself and ordered him away...it made him hard just thinking about it.

God, she was strong and smart and funny and beautiful. He loved her. He'd loved her from the moment he saw her. He was angry with her now, but he'd forgive her. There was no other option. Now that he had her, he couldn't live without her.

The garden was now everyone's favorite place, but he was pleased that it seemed to be empty for the moment. He wanted to seek Freya's council, and it would be good to check on the lass anyway. If news of Brachan's arrival had reached her, she was bound to have her own feelings about the revelation.

"Freya, lass. Where are ye?"

He turned the corner by the fountain as she stepped into view.

"Over here, lad. I doona believe Nicol will be down here this evening."

Maddock looked into Freya's eyes, but they gave nothing away. "Why do ye say that?"

She dipped her chin to look up at him from beneath her brows as she bent to sit at the edge of the fountain. "I know, Maddock. I've known for a verra long time."

"Ye what?"

She sighed as he sat down next to her. "Maddock, I am tied to Machara whether I wish to be or not. Much of what she feels is revealed to me. I've known that Brachan lived for as long as I've been here."

She'd known for all these years? Why did the women of this castle seem to feel the need to keep such secrets?

"And ye dinna tell him?"

"What good would that have done, lad? I dinna believe he would ever see the child. I saw no need to cause Nicol pain."

"But ye are his wife, Freya. There should be no secrets between ye."

Freya laughed, a full, loud laugh that echoed throughout the garden. "What fool told ye that, Maddock? Every person has their secrets. They are necessary, and often they are kind."

He frowned. "I'm not sure if I agree with ye, Freya."

"'Tis fine. I doona need ye to agree with me. Now." She gave his knee a pat, and as always, it passed right through him. "I can see that there is something that troubles ye. Go and work it out with her, lad. 'Tis never good to stay angry with those we love."

CHAPTER 36

I woke in the middle of the night to Maddock's body pressed against mine, his lips kissing me along my jaw.

"Kate, I need to tell ye something. Please, lass, wake up."

My eyelids fluttered open in the darkness. "Mm? What is it?"

"In truth, 'tis two things, but I willna tell ye either until ye are rightly awake so I know ye heard me."

"But I was sleeping so well."

His hand trailed down my body, his thumb dragging across my stomach as his hand dipped between my legs to cup my center. I lifted my hips and groaned as I pushed against him, urging his fingers to move.

"I'll make it worth yer while, lass, but first..." He pulled his hand away. "We must talk."

I could see nothing. The room was pitch black, but I sat up in the darkness as I reached for his hand.

"That's cruel, Maddock, to tease me that way."

"'Tis not teasing ye if I mean to make good on my promise."

211

"Well, good. Just tell me whatever you need to so you can resume what you were doing."

He kissed me softly in the darkness, and I smiled against his lips.

"I'm sorry, lass. I wish ye'd had more faith in me, but I canna fault ye for keeping the word ye gave to another. I shouldna have raised my voice to ye. I willna do it again."

I leaned forward to search for his lips so I could kiss him.

"Thank you for that. I accept your apology. What's the second thing?"

"I love ye. I love ye so much it hurts. I love ye in a way I dinna know 'twas possible."

I was grateful for the darkness. It kept him from seeing the tears flooding my cheeks.

"Do you really?"

He reached for me in the darkness, pulling me close to him as he wrapped his arms around me. "I do, lass. I love ye now, and I verra much expect I shall love ye forever."

I kissed him again and slipped my own hand down to latch onto him.

"I love you, too. Now, it's time for you to make good on your word."

There was a knock on the door early the next morning, but I stayed in bed as Maddock hurried to dress himself so he could answer the door.

I expected it to be one of the members of The Eight simply coming to chide Maddock for skipping his morning duties. When I heard Nicol's voice, I scrambled to pull the blankets over me as he stepped into the room.

"I'm sorry to disturb the both of ye. Brachan and I spent the whole night talking. I think it only right that we give him a chance to prove himself. He wishes to see Machara, to show all of us that he can resist her. We will stay gathered in the stairwell, ready to intervene if necessary. We know Machara will try to bend him to her will. If he can resist her, we will dedicate ourselves to finding a way to free him from her."

At least Nicol's time with Brachan had produced some sort of productive plan.

Maddock seemed to agree. "'Tis a good plan, Nicol. How are ye?"

There was a short pause then Nicol answered softly, "I am sad that I missed time with him. I doona doubt the lad's heart. I just doona know if anyone with such ties to Machara can resist her. But Maddock, he has one condition for appearing before Machara."

"Which is?"

"He will only do so if Kate stands by his side."

Maddock slammed the door in Nicol's face.

CHAPTER 37

"I know that I canna tell ye not to go with him, but I wish ye wouldna do so. I've seen what Machara can make another do. Calder was a good man before Machara gained control of him. He fought, he raged against her, but he was powerless to resist all that she called him to do."

I appreciated Maddock's worry, but there was no way I wasn't going to follow Brachan down into the dungeon. If he needed me, I was happy to be at his side.

I also couldn't help but wonder if this was how I was meant to defeat her? Could my belief in Brachan, my support of him, be enough to help him resist her, and as a result be the way that I was meant to fulfill my part in her destruction? Could it really be so simple?

I doubted it, but I was certainly willing to try.

"I have to, Maddock. Brachan won't go down there without me, and none of this will be over until he stands before his mother and faces her once and for all."

He paced the room as I dressed. "We should wait a few days. Try and prepare ye. Try and prepare him."

With my dress pulled up to my shoulders, I turned my back toward Maddock so he could help me with the laces.

"We can't wait, Maddock. Every day that passes it is more difficult for Brachan to resist her. To delay would only decrease his chances of defeating her. We should do this, and we should do this now."

hings came together quickly. Sydney and her crew would leave via Morna's magic and Mom and David would go into the village for safety, in case things turned south here at the castle.

Once all those not directly involved in the plan were away for the day, we gathered in Nicol's room so we could all go down into the dungeon together.

Brachan was already inside when I got there, standing with his back toward the doorway. I walked over and placed a gentle hand on his arm.

"Hey." He twisted to look at me, his eyes weary. "You don't look so good."

"I doona feel good, lass. My head aches dreadfully, and I feel like an arse."

"Why do you feel like that?"

"I shouldna be asking ye to do this for me. But ye are the only one here who believes I can resist her. I...I need ye, Kate."

I lifted my hand to his cheek and cupped it gently.

He looked so young, his eyes desperate and worried, but I knew he probably wasn't much younger than me.

"It's fine. I don't mind doing this. And you *can* resist her. I know you can. Are you ready to do this?"

The rest of The Eight were now gathered inside Nicol's room. There was no reason to wait any longer.

"Aye, lass. I'm ready."

---

*M*achara said nothing as Brachan stepped into view, and she didn't even seem to notice me as I moved over beside him.

She took her time looking him up and down. My heart ached for him as she did so.

She didn't look at him as if he were her son. She looked at him as if he were a thing—a tool she meant to use for her amusement.

When she did speak, there was no love in her voice for him. "Ye certainly take after yer father, lad. The fae is barely visible in ye. Mayhap a little in yer eyes, but if ye dinna know to look for it, ye wouldna know."

"Thank Brighid for that. Ye mean nothing to me, Machara. I want nothing to do with anything ye have planned for me. I willna harm my father. Nor will I harm the men who placed ye here."

She laughed and flicked her wrist as Brachan dropped to his knees. He screamed and covered his ears with his hands. The sound of Machara's laughter grew to other-worldly levels.

When she spoke again, her voice was different—booming, and scary as hell. "Can ye not see, lad? Ye doona have a choice. Ye are mine, and ye will do as I bid. Grab the lass next to ye, Brachan. Wrap yer hands around her neck and twist until it snaps."

He turned toward me, and his eyes were filled with a plea. I kneeled in front of him and tried to keep my eyes locked with his.

"Block it out, Brachan. You are not hers. You are the person you want to be—your mother's son, your real mother, the one who raised you. You are Nicol's son. You were raised in goodness, and goodness is what is in your heart."

He nodded as if he understood, but his hands shook as he pulled them away from his ears. He began to sob as he spoke, "I'm so sorry, lass. I doona want to hurt ye."

He lunged, but Maddock was on him before he could reach me. In an instant the other men pulled him away, chaining him with magic as they hauled him from the dungeon.

Machara's laugh echoed through the castle for hours.

CHAPTER 38

*I*n my opinion, the men overreacted to the entire situation. Brachan had lunged, but I'd never felt frightened. I believe he would've been able to stop himself. And it only took a moment after they pulled him away for him to gain composure of himself once again.

Compared to Brachan, I was frantic. As they dragged him up the stairs, I ran after them, pulling on the arms of any of the men I could reach, trying to get their attention as I begged them not to hurt him.

It was Nicol who'd finally been able to calm me by reaching out to grip my shoulder with his hand.

"I canna kill him, lass. I willna let them harm him. I doona know what we shall do, but I canna end his life."

Assured that Brachan was at least free from physical harm, I decided that the most useful thing I could do was to spend the day in the library and look through books to see if I could stumble across some way to help him. But I found nothing, and at some point in the day, I fell asleep with my head in a book.

"Lass, ye had me scared to death. I looked all over the castle

BETHANY CLAIRE

for ye." Maddock lifted me from my hunched position and gathered me in his arms like a child. He looked weary and sad.

"I'm sorry." I yawned as my eyes opened. "I fell asleep. I was looking for something that might help."

"Did ye find anything?"

"No." I lay my head into his chest as I struggled to remember my dream. It felt important that I not let it slip away.

"Where are ye, lass? Ye appear verra far away."

"I'm trying to remember something. I was dreaming about the book I read back home. About…I think it was about Calder." I could see bits of the text flash before my eyes as Maddock carried me up the stairs. I tried to recall what it said. "Oh my God!"

I tapped his shoulder so he would set me down.

"Maddock, I know what it was."

He lowered me, his expression curious. "What was it, lass?'

"Calder fell in love with a fae, yes? And that fae was turned into a human. Perhaps we can find a way to make Brachan fully human—to remove the fae from him."

"Ye do remember what happened to the lass Calder fell in love with, aye? She couldna bear her humanness once she had it. She threw herself from a cliff."

"Yes, but Brachan isn't fully fae. Even Machara admitted that he has more of Nicol than her within him. He would be able to survive it because he already thinks of himself as human."

He stepped away and crossed his arms skeptically. "He may be more human than fae, but he still has magic, lass. If 'twas stripped from him, 'twould be a terrible loss."

"I think it's a price he would be willing to pay to be free of Machara."

Maddock shrugged. "Mayhap so, but even if 'twas possible, Machara would never do it."

I had an idea. One I knew Maddock would hate. "Maybe we don't need Machara."

"I know of no other fae, lass."

I smiled and Maddock's expression immediately grew concerned. "I do. Machara's father. He hates Machara. Perhaps we could get him to remove the fae from Brachan."

"Lass, how do ye expect us to find him?"

"Machara will tell us. You already told me yourself. She thinks she's unbeatable. She won't mind telling me because she doesn't think it will matter."

Maddock took my hand and began to walk in the direction of Nicol's bedchamber. "I suppose there will be no talking ye out of this, aye lass?"

I shook my head and smiled. "None."

"Then we shall do it together."

CHAPTER 39

"Mayhap yer braver than I believed. I nearly had him kill ye, yet ye've come to see me again."

Maddock and I stood side by side, but this time as we faced her, Maddock allowed me to speak for myself.

"Machara, I need you to tell me where your father is."

"My father? What could ye possibly want with him?" Her tone was decidedly more intrigued than angry.

"I want to go to him and ask him if he will make Brachan fully human like you did with Calder's faerie lover."

She lifted a brow as she tilted her chin up. "Why would ye not ask me?"

"I'm no fool, Machara. I know you would never do that for Brachan."

"Ye are a fool if ye wish to go anywhere near my father, lass. He will either kill ye, woo ye, or keep ye in the land of the fae until ye are old and wilted."

Perhaps she was right. But this was the part I was meant to play in Machara's possible defeat. I could feel it in my bones. While I didn't know Machara's father, I didn't believe he would

223

kill me. If what her father wanted more than anything in the world was his daughter's demise, why wipe out the woman destined to play a role in that very demise?

Machara, of course, didn't know that.

"Then what do you have to lose by telling me?"

"Not a thing, lass. 'Twill be my pleasure to send ye to yer death. Near the Isle's far shore, two rivers meet. There is a hill, and on the other side is a clearing. Father dwells there in the land of the Fae. If he decides to see ye, he will make himself known to ye."

$\mathcal{M}$addock and I had to wait until the middle of the night to speak with Brachan. The men, unsure of what to do with him, locked him away in the room where they'd held Calder, and each took turns keeping watch over him. Maddock had the midnight watch, and I waited until his shift was halfway over before I made my way down to the room.

"Doona speak with him long, lass. If he agrees to do this, we shall approach the others with yer plan, but for now, we canna risk another one of the men coming along and seeing ye."

Nodding, I kissed him gently before stepping into the small, dark room where Brachan sat tied to a chair.

"You could break free from them if you wished, couldn't you?"

I grabbed one of the candles near the doorway so that he could see my face as I approached him.

"Kate, lass. Ye have to know I dinna mean to hurt ye. I..."

I reached out to touch his knee. "I know that. Don't worry. That's not why I'm here. So...you could break free if you wanted to, couldn't you?" I was attempting to lighten his mood, and it pleased me that he smiled just a little.

"Aye, lass, but I've no wish to be free. They are right to keep me locked away."

"Listen, I have an idea. If there was a way to turn you fully human—to remove any of the fae from you—would you take it?"

He didn't hesitate, as I'd predicted. "Aye. I feel more of me disappearing every day. A fortnight ago, I loved my life, lass. All I want is to have it back."

"I think we should go and look for your grandfather and ask him to help."

"Fae canna be trusted, lass."

"I know, but in this case, I truly believe we have the upper hand."

"Anything ye need me to do, lass, I will do."

CHAPTER 40

I tried to convince the men of my plan all on my own. We decided that would be best. That way, if they dismissed it or wouldn't agree to help, they wouldn't be suspicious of allowing Maddock to guard Brachan.

They turned me down flat. Even though the best suggestion any of them had was to just keep him bound up for the foreseeable future.

It didn't matter. My option was the best one.

If Laurel was here, I knew she would agree.

Come daybreak, Maddock and I were breaking him out.

This time tomorrow, I had every intention of being able to say I was the second woman to put a chink in that bitch's armor.

CHAPTER 41

*J*ust before dawn, when Maddock's shift was set to end, Maddock released Brachan, and we made our way out of the castle as quietly and quickly as possible.

We saw no one on the way out of the castle, in the stables, or along the path leading to the castle gates. It gave me hope that the rest of the morning would go just as smoothly.

We took two horses to the clearing. Brachan had his own, and I rode with Maddock on Stella. The ride was somber, as each of us seemed to be in our own worlds of worry.

It was a sunny day and warmer than any I'd experienced since arriving. Surely, that had to be a good omen.

Maddock knew the exact location of the place Machara had mentioned. He wasn't surprised that it was the place where Machara's father lived. He'd always thought it had a different feel to it—that I would be able to see what he meant when we arrived.

It didn't take us long to reach the hill before the clearing. No place on the Isle was very difficult to get to.

Midway up the hill, he dismounted and tied our horses so we could make the rest of the journey on foot.

"We need to prepare here, lass. There is no way to know how quickly after entering the clearing he will choose to appear."

"How do you mean?"

As far as I could tell, this entire thing was just going to require a whole lot of luck and wit. Words were important with faeries—I would have to watch every word that came out of my mouth.

Maddock and I walked hand-in-hand, with Brachan on the other side of me. He reached out to gently touch my shoulder so I would stop.

"There is a reason why there are so many stories of mortals falling for members of the fae, lass. The fae doona know how to relate to all that mortals feel, so they rely on their ability to manipulate yer baser instincts."

Maddock released my hand to step in front of me so that I was looking at both of them.

"He's right, lass. 'Tis possible he will try to take ye as his own. Ye will have to resist him."

Faerie charm was the last thing I was worried about. "Guys, I don't think that's going to be a problem. Your grandfather has to be like a thousand years old, right? I'm not going to be wooed by any faerie."

Maddock completely ignored me as he turned to look at Brachan. "Do ye have the ability to sway her, lad?"

He nodded. "Aye, but ye willna like it."

"Do it. She needs to see how overwhelming the sensation can be. Just a little, lad. Doona truly touch her."

I stood as still as I could as I watched Brachan saunter toward me. He stopped when our chests were nearly touching and gently leaned down to whisper in my ear.

"Do ye want me, lass?"

I snickered at the feeling of having his lips so close to my ear. "I am quite fond of you, Brachan, but no, I don't."

A warm stream of air suddenly swept over my ear, and the need that shot through me was crippling. I could feel my legs begin to shake, and it shocked me to realize that what I wanted more than anything was for Brachan to reach out and pull me toward him.

"What about now, lass?"

"Okay, okay." I held my hand up and stepped away from him. "I get it. Please stop."

As quickly as the sensation had come, it was gone.

"God, that's creepy."

"If a true fae decides to woo ye, lass, 'twould be ten times worse."

I regretted my earlier statement. I wasn't sure I would be able to resist any sensation that was much stronger than what Brachan had just caused me to feel.

"Why would he want to do that?"

"To idle yer mind so that whatever bargain ye strike with him holds no real benefit to ye."

I'd been frightened the moment this foolish idea popped into my mind, but now I was truly terrified. "Is there not anything I can do to resist that? To keep my mind clear?"

Maddock reached for me and pulled me into his arms. "Ye must find that place inside ye that benefited ye for so long. Seek the distraction, seek that place that keeps ye from feeling. Keep yer mind busy so he canna find his way in."

Surely, I could do that. I'd only been letting feelings in for a few days now. That coping mechanism couldn't be all that far away.

Brachan reached out to touch my back, and with Maddock's arms still around me, I twisted to look at him.

"'Tis time, lass. The other men are most assuredly already out looking for us. We must enter the land of the fae before they arrive. I will give the two of ye a moment. I'll wait for ye at the top of the hill."

Maddock said nothing until Brachan was a good distance away. When he did speak, his voice broke. "Kate, lass. I'm trying to stay strong, but I doona want ye to do this. Too many things could go wrong. I willna be able to bear it if ye doona come back to me."

I kissed his cheek and cupped his face with my palm.

"I have to do this. This is my part in all of this. I have no doubt of that. I want Brachan to be free of her, and one day, I want you to be free, as well. You'll never be if I don't play my part."

"I want to marry ye, lass." He said it so casually, I almost missed it.

"You what?"

"I want to marry ye. The moment ye return, I want us to leave here and get married. To run away together, just ye and me. What do ye say, lass?"

Eloping had always been my dream. But there was no way he could've possibly known that. "I say yes. As soon as I'm back, I will marry you."

"Then I shall wait, lass. Please doona let them keep ye there for years."

"Years?" Just the thought filled me with terror. "I don't plan to stay there for lunch, Maddock. I will not be there for years."

"'Tis what faeries do, lass. Doona be surprised if time is part of the bargain he tries to strike with ye."

I nodded, but my mind was now elsewhere. I needed Maddock's word that he wouldn't come in after me.

"I need you to make me a promise, Maddock. You have to promise me that you won't go in after me, no matter what. We have no way of knowing what Machara's father will do, and we can't risk one of The Eight ending up dead. There's only seven of you living. If another one of you dies, Machara breaks free. Do you understand? You have to promise."

He nodded and closed his eyes sadly as he gave his word. "I promise, lass. Now, kiss me and go before I decide I doona have the strength for this and pull ye away from here. Right now, I doona think I am above leaving Brachan to deal with this on his own."

"That's not an option. But I will kiss you. I'll kiss you now. I'll kiss you when I return. And I'll kiss you every day after. Everything is going to be fine, Maddock. I just know it."

I hoped it wasn't a lie. Something deep inside suspected it might be.

CHAPTER 42

What had he done? Why had he promised her that he wouldn't follow after her? It was all he wanted to do.

The worry over her would surely kill him. And if anything happened to her—well, he couldn't bear to think of it.

The rest of the men would be here soon enough, and who knew what would happen then. It was possible that they wouldn't let his betrayal stand. While they couldn't sever his bond to The Eight now, as soon as they found a man to replace Calder, they could.

He didn't care.

He'd seen in Kate's eyes that there'd be no dissuading her from this plan, and he'd rather help however he could than leave her to face such evil alone.

"Where have they gone? Ye have no time. Ye must go now."

Maddock jumped at the voice and quickly turned to see Paton step from the brush behind him.

"Are ye alone?"

"Aye. Though not for long. The others are on their way. I saw ye leave, and I heard the others discover ye were gone. I followed ye so I could warn ye that yer out of time. Ye must try and get to the land of the fae before the others arrive."

Paton's words surprised him. He'd been one of the first to question Kate's faith in Brachan.

"Are ye saying that ye came to help? Ye doona mean to try and stop us?"

"Aye. I knew the moment Kate told us of her plan that it dinna matter what we said to her. She meant to do it anyway. The more I thought on it, the more sense it made. But where are she and Brachan now?"

He pointed up the hill as he listened to his heart beat heavy in his throat.

"They've gone, Paton. They've gone to seek entry to the land of the fae."

"Then what the hell are ye doing here, Maddock? Why dinna ye go with them? She's no powers. She will be defenseless against any fae."

"I promised her that I wouldna go."

"Ye what?"

"She needs to do this alone, Paton. 'Tis her battle to fight and hers alone."

There was a sudden flash of light and the air around them seemed to turn as a translucent veil appeared at the top of the hill.

Maddock watched with horrified eyes as Paton took off at a sprint toward the opening to the land of the fae.

"I promised her nothing, and the lass' mother already hates me. If we let her die, I'll be unable to show my face at the castle ever again."

"Wait." He tried to catch him, but Paton had always been

fast. "Ye doona understand. Paton, none of The Eight can go through. If we die…"

It was too late, Paton threw himself through the veil and vanished before Maddock could finish.

Maddock dropped to his knees in despair. If Machara's father killed Paton, Machara would be free. And every last one of them would be dead.

I knew this clearing. It had been what I'd dreamed of so many nights ago in Laurel's apartment. And the man beside me, whose face had been blurry before, was now clear. I'd dreamed all of this. And now it was coming true.

We walked carefully into the clearing, for even the flowers seemed to be watching us. Machara's father knew we were here. I could sense it. With every step we took, the land around us was changing. In the distance, a throne appeared—the same one from my dreams, but this time, it wasn't empty.

While undoubtedly ancient, the man didn't look it. If I didn't know that he'd existed for, if not centuries, millennia, I'd have thought him not much older than Brachan. While his basic features were humanlike, he bore even less resemblance to humans than Machara. I found him terrifying to look at, and I had to strain every muscle in my legs to keep them from trembling.

"The lass may come forward. My grandson will not take another step. I'll not speak to him, nor do I wish to look upon him. He is an abomination, a creature who should not exist."

I glanced at Brachan uncomfortably, but he didn't seem wounded by the old faerie's words.

He winked at me, and something in the gesture gave me strength.

Slowly, I stepped forward.

It was time for me to see if I was worthy enough to play a part in Machara's demise.

CHAPTER 43

"Ye are frightened, lass. Ye needn't be."

I took each step toward the faerie slowly, as I hoped the long trek would give me enough time to read his face.

He stood as I neared the throne, and I swallowed hard as he billowed up at least eight feet when fully straight.

"I doona speak in jest, lass. Ye can breathe and let go of yer worry. I'll not harm ye. Nor will I harm Brachan."

For the first time since seeing him, I spoke. "I'm not worried about you harming me. Why would you harm one of the women meant to destroy your daughter? I'm worried about you harming Brachan."

He stepped down from his throne and walked toward me, offering me his hand to help me up the steps.

Reluctantly, I took it. The flesh of his fingers was smooth and wet, like that of a dolphin. It unsettled me, but then again, everything about him was unsettling.

"Precisely, lass. I'll bring no harm to Brachan. Even if I may want those of my blood dead, I canna bring myself to end their lives myself. I simply create a way for someone else to end them for me."

"Why? It's still your hand in it—that is no different than doing it yourself."

He shrugged and released my hand as he resumed his place on his throne. "Mayhap so, but it allows my conscience to be free."

"I didn't know you all had one of those."

He bit his lower lip and anger flashed in his eyes. "There is much ye doona know, lass. Much ye never will. Come. Sit down." A stool appeared beside him out of nowhere. Hesitantly, I moved toward it. "Tell me why ye have come."

"Why do you want your daughter dead? What did she do to make you hate her so much?"

"She betrayed me. She betrayed her family. For centuries, the fae lived on this Isle unknown to mortals. Machara was the first to open the veil between yer land and ours. Her choice has only brought pain and destruction to both our species. Now." His long fingers wrapped around the arms of his chair, and his knuckles grew white as he squeezed it. He was quickly losing his patience with me. "Enough of Machara. Why are ye here?"

"You want Machara dead, and I'm one of the women that can help make that happen, but there's a problem I don't think I can fix without you."

"Brachan." He said it as a matter of fact, not a question.

"Yes. Machara is bending him to her will, and he is unable to resist it. As long as fae blood runs within him, I stand no chance of surviving a fortnight."

"Why not just kill him, lass? 'Twould be the simplest solution."

I decided to give him the one reason I hoped would appeal to his desires more than any other. "Machara won't care if he's dead.

It would pain her so much more to know that the son she'd created was no longer hers to toy with. To see that she had no power over him, and he was his own man in every way."

The faerie smiled so wide I could see that his back teeth were just a series of points. It caused me to visibly shiver.

"I doona eat humans, lass, nor do I tup them. The propensity that some fae have for humans is one I've never shared."

I didn't even know how to respond to that. I decided to ignore the statement altogether. "Will you help me?"

"Aye, though surely ye must know faeries do nothing without a bargain. What do ye offer me in return?"

"What is it that you want?"

He smiled again and stood to pace back and forth in front of me as he thought. "There is nothing ye have that I want, lass. Ye are mortal. Ye are worthless. But mayhap, at another time, ye would be useful."

Something on the edges of my brain was getting fuzzy. It wasn't the erotic brain-drain that Brachan made me feel. It was something else, just a general sense of lackluster, something that made it difficult for me to care. "What are you doing?"

"I'm not harming ye, lass. I already told ye I'd not do that."

Apathy was overtaking me. I should've felt hyper-alert, worried for Brachan, for myself, for whatever deal this man intended to force me to make, but all I felt was disinterest.

"You may not be causing me physical harm, but you're not playing fair."

He laughed and stopped in front of me, leaning so close I could feel his breath. Its odor was sweet and sickly. "I never said anything about being fair, lass. Now, let us continue. Ye have nothing I need now, but that doesna mean I am unwilling to bargain with ye. Take my hand. I will free ye from here, and I will see Brachan turned into the human he so desperately wishes to be. All I ask in return is that ye owe me a favor. At a time of my choosing, I may ask for yer help, and ye must agree to give it."

Some small part of my brain resisted it. I knew this was the worst promise I could ever make with a fae, but the right emotions just wouldn't come forward. I tried to do what Maddock suggested. I tried to shut down and distract my brain, but it was too late. He'd slipped in without me noticing and had forced his powers on me so quickly, I never had a chance.

He reached for my hand, and I didn't pull away, but just as his fingers began to brush against my own, a voice bellowed from the bottom of the throne.

"No, Kate! Doona do it."

The fae jerked back as if he'd been run through with something, and the expression of shock on his face was unmistakable. My apathy vanished in an instant—the fae's surprise was enough to cause him to break his hold over my mind. Jumping from my seat, I looked down to see Paton approaching Machara's father with fury in his eyes.

"She'll be making no bargain with ye. 'Tis cowardly of ye to bargain with someone who has no control over their mind. Bargain with someone immune to yer powers."

"How were ye here without me knowing it?" The fae was shaken. He was unable to hide it.

"We've magic, ye big, ugly arse. Unlike true mortals that ye can bend to yer will any time ye please, ye can only tamper with our minds if we've given ye our blood and I shall never give ye mine." Paton paused and glanced over at me. "Leave here, Kate. If there is a bargain to be made, I shall make it."

"No." It had to be me. Of this I was certain. If Paton stepped in, then my part in Machara's demise wouldn't be complete. "It has to be me, Paton. Otherwise, Machara can never be beaten."

He nodded, and I saw the reluctant acceptance settle in his gaze. "If ye insist, come and hold my hand so I may protect ye with my own magic. At least he willna be able to weaken yer mind as ye bargain with him."

I ran toward Paton, quickly taking his hand as the fae watched us with interest.

When my hand was safely wrapped up in Paton's, the fae spoke once more. "Fine. Let us bargain this way. It willna matter. Make me an offer, lass."

I couldn't offer him a favor. The one thing I could offer him was the one thing that would hurt me the most. The one thing that would break Maddock's heart.

"What if I offer you time? Make Brachan human. Swear to me that you won't harm me, nor age me, and you may keep me here for exactly three human years. Then you shall return me to the land of mortals, and you will never bother me again."

The fae smiled. I could see that my offer pleased him. He hated humans. He wouldn't accept because he wanted me there, but he would accept if he thought it might cause other humans pain.

"'Twill feel like a hundred years to ye, lass."

I nodded, my heart breaking as I resigned myself to my destiny.

Paton turned toward me and gripped my shoulder hard with his free hand.

"What are ye doing, lass? No mortal can survive spending so long in this realm. He doesna have to harm ye for it to destroy ye. Ye would never be the same once he released ye from here."

Tears began to run down my face, but I knew there was no turning back now.

"It doesn't matter. It's the only way, and someday you guys

have to be free." I paused and turned toward my soon-to-be captor. "What do you say?"

"If ye offer me yer hand, I will accept."

I waited and turned toward Paton one more time. "Tell Laurel I'm sorry, Paton. Tell my mom I love her. And tell Maddock I love him most of all. Tell him if he doesn't want to wait, I understand. Tell him that I'll do everything I can to hold onto myself while I'm here. And Paton, please take care of Crink. He..." I let out a sob as I collapsed into Paton's chest. "He won't understand."

Paton lifted me away from him, and with one of his hands still holding mine, he lifted his free hand and held up two fingers.

"I'm sorry for this, lass, but Maddock and yer mother would never forgive me if I dinna do it."

He slammed his fingertips hard into my chest, and I froze. I couldn't move, couldn't blink, couldn't do anything but watch on in horror as Paton turned to face the fae.

"I offer ye the same bargain. Make Brachan human, release him and Kate into the land of mortals immediately, unharmed, and the same age they are now, and ye may take me for the length of three human years. She willna benefit ye, but if I'm here, ye might study the power within me." He held out his hand, and the fae stepped forward. "Ye must decide now."

The moment Machara's father latched onto Paton's hand, my vision went black.

CHAPTER 44

I woke on the top of the hill, propped up in Nicol's arms. I could hear chanting to my left, and as I blinked myself awake, I turned to see what was happening.

"Doona worry, lass. Ye are safe."

"What are they doing? What's wrong? Where's Brachan?" I suddenly remembered Paton and broke down into tears. "Paton...he's...he..."

Nicol's arms were wrapped around me, and he gently rocked me as he spoke into my hair. "Shh, lass. We know. We know where Paton is. He did the only thing any of us could do."

"Is the...did his bond break with The Eight?"

Nicol nodded. "Aye, but Machara is not free. Brachan is human now, but by some miracle, his powers remain. The men are initiating him into The Eight now. We've still seven men."

*M*addock was quiet on the way back to the castle, and his thoughts were very far away.

I knew what he was thinking, and I hated it.

"Thank you, Maddock."

He sighed and kept his eyes ahead as he spoke. "For what, lass? For allowing my friend to sacrifice three years of his life for ye when I should've been the one to step inside and make such a bargain?"

"You allowed nothing. You have no more control over Paton's actions than you do over mine. All you did was keep your word, and it means the world to me."

Maddock let out a strained sob, and he pulled me toward him even more tightly.

"I shall never be able to repay him. He has given ye back to me, and he has given Brachan a new life, as well."

"He'll be okay, won't he?"

Maddock hesitated, but his tone was confident in his answer. "Aye. His magic will protect him. Better him stuck there than ye."

"I failed, Maddock." I whispered the words. "Paton saved Brachan, not me. We're no closer to defeating Machara than we were before. It seems I was wrong—I'm not one of the nine women meant to defeat her."

"I wouldna be so sure about that, lass. The moment ye and Brachan appeared at the top of the hill, ye lying there unconscious and Brachan fully human, the entire Isle shook from her screaming. She knows she was defeated once again. I believe ye've completed yer duty."

I could see the castle in the distance.

"I hope so. When we get back, she's the first person I want to see."

*H*and in hand, Brachan and I made our way down to the dungeon. The Machara I'd seen before was gone.

Curled up in the back corner of her cell, she wailed as we looked in at her.

I had nothing to say. I only wanted to see that my job was done.

It was Brachan who needed to make his peace with her. "I am free of ye, and I shall spend every day of my life until ye are good and truly dead making sure ye remain here. Ye are not my mother. Ye never were, and ye never will be."

Brachan didn't need to hear her response. Turning, he led me from the dungeon as we closed the door on our part of Machara's story.

CHAPTER 45

One Week Later

"Maddock...oh God, Maddock. I can't...I can't..." I screamed as I unraveled beneath his tongue. He quickly rose to kiss my neck as he plunged inside me. I wouldn't have thought it possible to climax again so quickly, but it took no time for me to meet his passion once again.

"Do ye still want to marry me, lass?"

I couldn't begin to fathom how he was capable of speech at this moment. "What?"

"Tell me..." He groaned as he pumped inside me. "Tell me ye still wish to marry me."

"Of course I do."

"Good." He thrust deep into me once more. As he found his release, he slowly came down on top of me, kissing along my jaw as he spoke. "I've a surprise for ye."

"Oh yeah? What's that?"

"I've a bath drawn for ye in yer mother's cottage. Ye needn't dress. I've laid out a robe for ye to wear on yer way. They will tell ye more when ye get there."

I was so happily sated, all I wanted to do was sleep.

"Do I need to go now? Can we nap for a little bit first?"

He flipped me on my side and gave my butt a gentle swat. "No, ye must go now. There is no time to waste."

⁂

*M*om stood outside the cottage she now shared with David, grinning like a fool, as I walked up the pathway in my robe. She was bouncing on her feet with excitement.

"What is going on, Mom?"

She waved me toward her. "Come in and you'll see."

Eyeing her suspiciously, I walked into the cottage and looked at the sight before me.

A warm bath stood in the middle of the room, a gorgeous and entirely modern wedding gown hung on a hook on one wall, and two people I'd certainly not expected to see today—Laurel and Morna—stood at the back of the room.

"Happy wedding day!" Laurel beamed at me as she ran across the room to throw her arms around my neck.

"Is it? Laurel, what are you doing here?"

She grabbed my hand as she stepped away. "Yes, it is your wedding day. Maddock told us you agreed to marry him and that you'd already agreed to elope, but surprising you with the day is part of the fun. As for my being here...let's just say that Raudrich's powers were giving him a bit of a read on what was going on here. Needless to say, he was a bit too anxious to enjoy our time away. Not that it matters, I was happy to come home, too."

I looked over at Morna who was smiling as she opened her arms to me. "And what are you doing here?"

"There is no rule that I canna use my magic for love. I brought the dress, and once ye are ready, I shall send ye to the location of yer wedding."

"Which is?"

She tsked at me and shook her head. "Ach, I canna tell ye that. Maddock would never forgive me. Now, let's get ye ready."

*I*t was a scary thing to let someone send you hurtling from one location to another while blindfolded, but I trusted Morna enough that I managed to keep it together as she sent us zipping through time.

When we landed on our feet, Maddock's voice spoke to me from behind. "Ach, lass. I can see why ye dreamed of this place. I dinna know such light could exist."

I gasped as a small glimmer of hope surged through me. "No! We're not...Maddock, where are we? You have to tell me right now."

His hands moved to the knot on the back of my blindfold. When he lifted it from my eyes, I looked down on the city of Paris from the top of a tourist-free Eiffel Tower, and I began to cry.

"Maddock, how did you know? I...I always wanted to get married here."

He smiled and reached up to dab my tears with his thumb. "I asked yer mother when I asked for her blessing. Are ye happy, lass?"

I kissed him, not minding at all that my makeup was definitely ruined. "I've never been so happy in my life."

We were married by a stranger, and our witness was one of the light technicians for the tower.

With the help of Morna's magic, my out-of-time Scot and I spent the evening on blankets laid out for us on the top of the most beautiful structure in the world, overlooking the most beautiful city.

Our wedding day was perfect in every way, and I had no doubt that our life together would be just as wonderful as this special day.

EPILOGUE

*A*llen Territory

"*T*here's a letter for ye, mistress."

Silva ran toward the messenger, quickly pulling the letter from his hand. "Thank ye."

She broke the wax seal quickly as she frantically read the message she'd been awaiting for far too long.

Dear Silva,

I am sorry we didn't have much time to speak at the wedding, but thank ye for coming. It meant more than you know.

I didn't forget my promise to you, and I believe I have found just the man to take over your duties for the territory. He arrives in a fortnight.

And then you are free.

Come and visit us at the Isle. You are welcome any time.

Your friend,
     Raudrich

She was free. Finally, she could move on from a place that brought her only grief.

THE END

Thank you for reading *Love Beyond Wanting*. I hope you enjoyed it! If you did...

1. Help other people find this book by **writing a review.**
2. Sign up for my **newsletter**, to be notified of my new releases. Just visit my website and click on the **mailing list** link in the header.
3. Like my **Facebook** page.
4. Visit my website: **www.bethanyclaire.com**

To continue the series, read:

Love Beyond Destiny

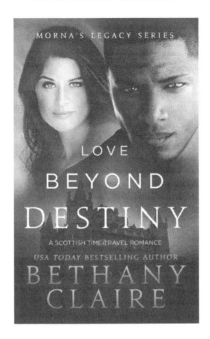

Sweet/Clean Version of *Love Beyond Compare*

Morna's Ghost
Sweet/Clean Version of *Love Beyond Dreams*

Morna's Vow
Sweet/Clean Version of *Love Beyond Belief*

The McMillans' Magical Yuletide
Sweet/Clean Version of *A McMillan Christmas*

Morna's Turn
Sweet/Clean Version of *Love Beyond Reach*

SUBSCRIBE TO BETHANY'S MAILING LIST

When you sign up for my mailing list, you will be the first to know about new releases, upcoming events, and contests. You will also get sneak peeks into books and have opportunities to participate in special reader groups and occasionally get codes for free books.

Just go to my website (www.bethanyclaire.com) and click the Mailing List link in the header. I can't wait to connect with you there.

ABOUT THE AUTHOR

BETHANY CLAIRE is a USA Today bestselling author of swoon-worthy, Scottish romance and time travel novels. Bethany loves to immerse her readers in worlds filled with lush landscapes, hunky Scots, lots of magic, and happy endings.

She has two ornery fur-babies, plays the piano every day, and loves Disney and yoga pants more than any twenty-something really should. She is most creative after a good night's sleep and the perfect cup of tea. When not writing, Bethany travels as much as she possibly can, and she never leaves home without a good book to keep her company.

If you want to read more about Bethany or if you're curious about when her next book will come out, please visit her website at: www.bethanyclaire.com, where you can sign up to receive email notifications about new releases.

Connect with Bethany on social media, visit her website for lots of book extras, or email her:
www.bethanyclaire.com
bclaire@bethanyclaire.com

ACKNOWLEDGMENTS

To Marsha Bredeson, Rori Bumgarner, Karen Corboy, Elizabeth Halliday, Johnetta Ivey, Vivian Nwankpah, and Pamela Oviatt, thank you so much for your work on this book.

To Mom and Maegan, thanks for keeping me sane and cheering me on during those last few late nights.

Made in the USA
Middletown, DE
10 June 2022